RANCHER UNDER FIRE

BARB HAN

TORJAKE PUBLISHING

Editing: Ali Williams

Cover Design: Jacob's Cover Designs

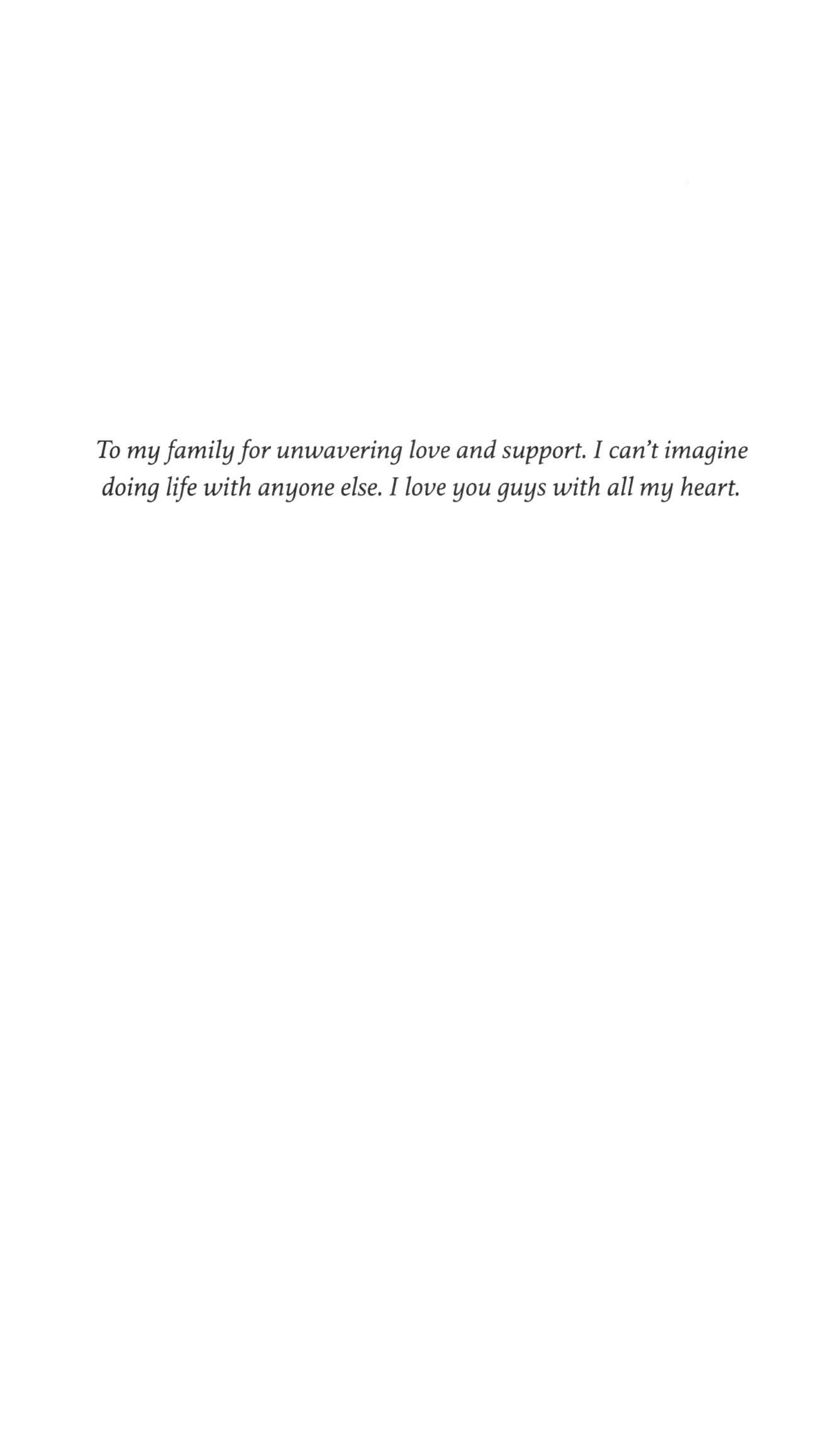

To my family for unwavering love and support. I can't imagine doing life with anyone else. I love you guys with all my heart.

1

A dead raccoon. A moment of panic. An SOS text.

Those three things in succession brought Liv Holden's past knocking; Corbin Firebrand stood on her porch. She didn't want to need him as much as she did. Seeing him again caused an unexpected physical reaction. Her throat dried up, her stomach tingled, and her heart free fell. Taking a fortifying breath, she opened the door.

"Before you say anything, I didn't know who else to call." She put a hand up and winced, steadying herself for the verbal blows that seemed sure to come based on the look on his face.

"Why not try your husband?" Corbin asked, tension radiated off him in palpable waves. It was late June and already hot enough outside with adding to the rising temperature.

"Ex," she quickly added. "And I'm not trying to put you in a bad position here."

"Really?" Corbin rocked back on his boot heels. "Because last time I checked, you were still married to my cousin."

"And you used to be my best friend," she shot back. This probably wasn't the time to point out the fact Kellan Firebrand was probably Corbin's least favorite cousin and always had been. Those two had butted heads for as long as she could remember. Or the reality that he'd been sending her threatening texts and there wasn't a person in town who would take her side over his.

"You've been gone for a year," he stated. "Why come back now, and why text me?"

"I don't want to be here anymore than half the town wants me to be." The breath she blew out was meant to calm her but shot up her blood pressure instead.

He cocked an eyebrow. "What did you think would happen when you came back? A welcome wagon? A parade?"

"I didn't think people would turn against me." She could hear the defensiveness in her own tone. She stepped outside, bent over the dead raccoon, and lifted the towel enough for Corbin to see underneath. She immediately let go and pulled her hand back. Bile burned the back of her throat at the sight of the poor animal. Her heart nearly broke in half. "I didn't think someone would play a sick prank like this one."

Corbin muttered the same curse she was thinking. He bent down and examined the creature. "No one deserves this, least of all this poor guy." A few more of those choice words slipped out of his mouth before he looked up at her. "Kellan did this?"

"No idea. I'd like to believe he isn't capable but after his hateful messages, I'm not so sure," she admitted. Liv twisted her hands together and diverted her gaze, unable to look at the cruelty any longer. "I'm sorry. No one else will return my calls and I—"

"Did the right thing by reaching out to me. I'll take care of it." Corbin shot her a warning look.

"For your information, I called Ronnie first," she said. Ronnie Patel worked for animal services. The cold shoulder treatment she was receiving from her former best friend hurt deeper than she wanted to show, so she forced her shoulders back and straightened her spine.

"And?" Corbin's gaze narrowed. Impatience edged his tone. His reaction was a knife stab, but she probably shouldn't have expected anything different.

"He said I should figure out a way to dispose of it myself. Said I was good at getting rid of things I didn't want anymore," she stated. Chin up, she refused to show how much the comment, and others like it, hurt.

Corbin studied her for a long moment and she couldn't tell if his anger was aimed at her at the injustice she'd suffered.

"Ronnie's a jerk," Corbin finally muttered.

"I don't need you to tell me that," she quipped. Lone Star Pass had been home her entire life—save for the past year—but living under a microscope was for the birds. She felt like an ant underneath a magnifying glass on the sidewalk in August when she ran errands like going to the grocery store or the bank.

Corbin hopped off the porch before making a roundtrip to his truck. As he strode back, he put on a pair of disposable gloves. He pulled a plastic bag from his back pocket and took care of the animal, trying off the bag and then setting it beside the porch.

"Come in for a cup of coffee?" Liv asked, expecting an express rejection. Considering how few friends she had in town, it was worth a try.

He studied her for a long moment like he was trying to

read her mind. Then, he removed the gloves and placed them on top of the bag.

"Okay," he finally said. "But I can't stay long."

"Doesn't take long to brew a pot." She opened the door and walked inside, half expecting him to turn around and head to his truck. He didn't and her heart stirred.

"What's up with the moving boxes?" Corbin looked around the kitchen. "Are you going somewhere?"

"I can't live here any longer, Corbin." She turned around and studied him, searching for the hatred she'd seen in the faces of several of his cousins when she'd passed by them in town. She'd been home less than a week and the chilly reception she'd received cut to the core.

"Because of a cruel joke?" he countered, stopped at the door to the kitchen and leaning into the doorjamb. "Don't get me wrong, I'm not diminishing what happened here. This is disgusting and someone needs to be made aware this is not okay. It's possible someone found the animal already deceased and threw it on your porch as a twisted joke."

"Is that all you think has been going on?" She smacked her flat palm against the granite countertop. "Yesterday morning I woke up to two of my tires being slashed, which made me late for an appointment."

Admitting it, saying the words out loud caused her chest to squeeze. She took in a few slow breaths to stave off the mounting panic attack at the fact the so-called jokes were escalating.

"What else?" The muscle in Corbin's jaw ticked, a sure sign his temper was flaring and he was doing his level best to keep it in check.

"Let's see. Lots of prank phone calls and awful texts. All from unknown numbers." She fished her cell from her back pocket and held it on the flat of her palm. She wasn't trying to rile him up further but, man, she needed to vent to someone. "Take a look and see for yourself if you don't believe me."

"This constitutes harassment," Corbin said, a fire raged in his eyes.

"You think so?" she asked sarcastically before she had a chance to reel the words back in. She shot him a look of apology. "I'm sorry. I'm not trying to take any of this out on you. I'm just frustrated and tired, and it breaks my heart this animal had to suffer. None of this was the raccoon's fault."

Corbin took a step closer, causing a dozen campfires to light inside her, warming places that got her into trouble with their friendship in the first place. He studied her and she could swear she felt his temperature rising. His gaze dropped to her phone.

"How long did you say this been going on?" His frustration looked like a simmering pot just before it boiled over.

"Ever since I got the final divorce papers to sign, which was basically the day I returned home." She dropped her gaze, unable to look him in the eye. Marrying his cousin had been a mistake she would regret the rest of her life for many reasons, not the least of which was losing Corbin. "Anyway, what are you going to do with that poor critter?"

"First of all, you're going to call Sheriff Lawler and report—"

"Oh no, I'm not. And you have to promise you won't tell anyone either," she countered. "I'm not stirring that pot. It's bad enough now. I can't even walk into the store without someone making a snide remark."

Chin to chest, Liv blinked away the tears threatening. No one got to make her cry again. And she sure didn't want Corbin to see her on the brink of losing it.

"The sheriff needs to know," Corbin pressed, softening

his tone—a tone that had a bad habit of washing over her and through her like the warmth from a fireplace on a cold night.

"And then what?" She cocked an eyebrow. "The hazing gets worse? I'm the one who ends up in a plastic bag?"

She shook her head before he could answer.

"No, thanks," she said. "I have a job interview in Dallas in two days. If I get that job, I'm out of here faster than you can point a finger and tell me I brought this on myself."

"I would never do that," he practically growled.

Maybe not right now. But you would eventually. And she wouldn't blame him.

CORBIN HAD HALF a mind to hop inside his pickup, kick up a little dust on the way out of here, and confront Kellan. This was low, even for his cousin, and there was no way Corbin planned to stand idly by and watch Kellan intimidate someone they both once cared about. His cousin was hurting. Corbin had seen it in the way he carried himself. Head down, shoulders forward, the man walked around like the wind had been knocked out of him. Even after a year, he'd only grown crankier. But this?

"I know what you're thinking, Corbin Firebrand," Liv said. He ignored the way her voice traveled all over his body, bringing light to places that had been dark for a long time.

"I seriously doubt it," he shot back. There had been a time when she might have been able to read his mind. Their connection died at the altar the day she wed Kellan.

"Suit yourself. But I've known you since the third grade and even then, the vein in your neck bulged when you were about to finish someone else's fight," she warned. "It's happening right now."

"Anyone could have guessed and been right. Doesn't prove anything and it doesn't take a rocket scientist or mind reader to realize I'd be angry about the possibility of someone killing an innocent animal or bullying someone who doesn't deserve it." Was he being defensive? Yes. And he'd scored a direct hit based on the hurt in her eyes. Good. He didn't want to be reminded how well they knew each other, and she couldn't afford to be. Based on what she'd just said, she was about to cut bait and move on.

He glanced at her ring finger just to confirm she wasn't wearing the stark reminder he didn't know her as well as he should have.

"Why come back now? It's been a year since you pulled your disappearing act," Corbin recalled.

"The divorce will be final as soon as I sign the papers." She moved to the coffee pot and went to work.

"As I understand it, you walked out. Why does it sound like you're the holdup?" Curiosity got the best of him and he had to ask. If he was smart, he'd finish what he came here to do and then get as far away from Liv as possible. From the sounds of it, she'd be gone in a few days once the job came through in Dallas. He could wash his hands of this whole sticky situation even though the thought of never seeing her again ripped a hole in his insides.

Liv clamped her mouth shut. This wasn't the time to get quiet on him.

"Let me guess, he's asking for something you don't want to give up?" It would be just like Kellan to find a way to punish her by taking away something she loved. Corbin had a few choice words for his cousin when this conversation was over. The man needed to get a grip and accept the fact the marriage was done. Yes, it was a harsh reality. Yes, it must hurt beyond anything Kellan had ever imagined. And yes, it had to be right up there with the most awful thing that could happen. But it was time to bite the bullet and move on.

"Bingo. Now, go collect your prize." She rolled her eyes and sighed a heavy sigh. "Coffee is ready if you want a cup."

"Don't you have to get to work or finish up here?" He glanced around at the half-filled boxes.

"Work on a Saturday? In these?" She motioned toward her jogging suit.

"How should I know? I haven't kept up with you in eighteen months," he countered.

She winced like she'd just taken a punch and guilt squeezed his chest. He stopped himself right there. She didn't need to be reminded he didn't care anymore, which wasn't even true. There was no shut-off valve for a Firebrand. But trying to be friendly now would only make walking away more difficult, and as much as he didn't care for Kellan, sneaking around behind his back wasn't an option. The two of them might not get along but there was a code when it came to family. Whether Corbin liked it or not, he had to cold-shoulder Liv. Giving her false hope they could somehow reconnect wasn't fair to either one of them.

"At least stay long enough to finish your cup." She double fisted a pair of mugs before turning to walk toward him.

"I already said that I—"

"Yeah? Well, guess what? I can't send you away looking like you're about to wring your cousin's neck. So, you might as well sit down and drink until you calm down." She compressed her lips, and a storm brewed behind those dark roast eyes of hers.

This probably wasn't the time to notice her heart-shaped face or that dimple on her chin he used to think was the cutest thing he'd ever seen. He would tease her about it when he wanted her to chase him around the playground as kids. Now, all he could think about was how his lips would feel there, peppering kisses toward her lips. Thick, full cherry lips that were set on skin so silky, so creamy he had to fist his hand to keep from reaching out to touch her. Liv had an unrivaled natural beauty and a heart of gold to match.

More reasons not to torture himself by sticking around.

But she'd made a good point about him needing a minute to calm down. Plus, she was rattled by what had happened and he'd be a jerk to walk away when she was this upset. What could finishing his cup of coffee hurt?

Famous last words, he thought.

"Fine." He walked to the table, pulled out a chair, and sat down.

"Fine," she parroted as she set the mugs down, turned away from him, and walked away. He forced his gaze off her sweet, round backside, glancing around the room instead. The stack of boxes struck him like a physical blow. This seemed like a good time to remind himself that what she did with her life wasn't any of his business, no matter how much that felt like a lie. *Heaven help him.*

"I hope you still take yours black," she said as she poured a few breakfast biscuits onto a plate and then brought it over to the table.

"Yes." He picked up his mug and took a sip, welcoming the burn on his throat. He still couldn't get over the fact someone had set out to...what...scare her? Intimidate her? Force her into doing something she didn't want to do?

She needed to agree to bring in the law and the main reason he was sticking around was to find a way to convince her. Family or not, Kellan shouldn't get to throw his weight around.

"Biscuit?" Liv asked, holding the plate toward him. He must've drawn back without realizing because she quickly added, "I don't bite." Then, she half smiled but he could still see the stress and tension in her eyes. "Aside from the time in fourth grade, but then you had it coming."

Their gazes connected a second too long at the memory. He couldn't afford to feel fondness toward her, so he shut down the emotion.

When he didn't respond, she cleared her throat and pushed the plate closer. "Here you go. It goes with the coffee."

As he took the offering, their fingers grazed. The electrical impulse that shot through him with the lightest contact was as unwelcomed as a hundred-and-ten-degree heat in August. Both caused devastation. With the two-year drought Lone Star Pass had been in, the coming months threatened to be deadly.

"Do you want to see what he's been writing to me?" She took a seat and pulled out her cell before setting it on the table. With two fingers, she pushed the piece of tech toward him.

Corbin skimmed the screen. Fire raced through his blood as he read the threats and name-calling. Kellan might be hurting but there was no defense good enough for this unacceptable behavior. Corbin shook his head and realized he'd fisted his hands.

"This is all the evidence you need to make this go away." He motioned toward the cell before lifting his gaze to hers. Her hair was shorter now, shoulder length and cut to frame her face. The auburn tint contrasted against her creamy skin and thick black lashes brought out the dark roast color in her eyes.

"You know why I can't do that," she insisted.

"Kellan needs to be sent a message." Corbin would do it himself if it would do any good. Taking his cousin to task over anything involving Liv might make the situation worse for her.

"Or I need to get through this and move on." She glanced around and her expression morphed from anger to sadness. "I'll miss this old place, though."

"Why leave at all? Stand your ground and keep your family home. People will get over themselves at some point and you won't have to uproot your entire life." The part of him that would miss her more than he cared to admit grabbed hold of the wheel for a few seconds there. He needed to rein it in because where she lived and what she did wasn't his business anymore.

"Sure sounds easy coming from you," she said before picking up a pencil and tapping the eraser on the wooden table.

"What is that supposed to mean?" he shot back.

"I think we both know being a Firebrand in this town stacks the deck for you as much as burning one pits the whole town against you." *Tap. Tap. Tap.*

He couldn't stop staring at the pencil.

Corbin could admit there was a whole lot of truth to what she'd just said. He knew all about the privilege that came with being a Firebrand. He also knew the other side of the coin—the side no one wanted to discuss. Living in Lone Star Pass with his last name came with a lot of expectations. It came with a father and uncle who were constantly feuding. And it came with a grandfather who'd been more than happy to sit back and watch the fireworks while he was alive.

Liv took a sip of coffee. She studied the rim of her mug like she was studying for finals. "That wasn't a fair statement and I apologize. You've never used your family name to get an advantage."

When she came at him with fire, he didn't feel like a jerk for pushing back. But understanding? Sympathy? Those emotions threatened to chip away at the ice encasing his heart where she was concerned.

"It's what everyone thinks anyway," he said, dismissing her comment like it was nothing.

"Doesn't mean it's right of me to say or think," she conceded.

"We're not here to talk about how easy or difficult my life is." He needed to guide the conversation back on track and think of a way to get her through the next couple of days. Because the day she'd married his cousin was the worst in Corbin's life and he had no plans to revisit that pain.

"I'm putting you in a bad position," she said, turning an about-face. "Enjoy your coffee, eat a biscuit, and then we'll call it a day."

"Doing that won't get Kellan to leave you alone if he's behind this," he countered. He was serious about helping her figure out a way to make it stop without him stepping in. Him going to Kellan would likely pour gasoline on the blaze. She'd been right about that.

"While you're here, can I ask you a personal question?" She absently ran her finger along the rim of the mug.

"Are you serious about leaving this place and never looking back if you get the job?" Maybe he could risk one last real conversation with Liv, as long as it really was that, the last. His chest squeezed at the thought of her leaving town and never coming back, and he tried his best to chalk it up to muscle memory.

She nodded.

"Then, shoot," he said.

She cocked her head to one side like she did when she felt vulnerable and damned if the move didn't strike him square in the chest.

"Why didn't you marry her?" she asked.

The question caught him off guard. He tried to hide his surprise but was afraid she would see right through him. But they had nothing to gain from him answering the question.

2

Corbin set his cup of coffee on the table. One look at him, mouth clamped shut and gaze narrowed, told Liv he had no intention of answering her question. And yet, his proposal to Dani had turned Liv's life upside down.

The sound of a vehicle coming up the drive caught both of their attention. Corbin stepped outside using the back-door while muttering something about putting an end to this nonsense. She followed close on his heels, figuring she might need to jump in the middle.

"What's Ed Roberts doing here?" Corbin put a hand out to stop her from going around him. Was protective instinct causing him to make sure he stood in between her and Ed?

"I ran into his wife at the store a few weeks ago when I came home to check on the house. He's been hounding me ever since. Wants to list my family's house," Liv said.

"So, you've been thinking about moving away from Lone Star Pass for a while now?" he asked.

The question caught her off guard. He must realize her life here was over the minute she walked away from Kellan.

"Yes. Like I told you. This town is not friendly to anyone who is marked the enemy of a Firebrand." The past year since leaving town had been the loneliest of her life. Every time she'd come back to check on the house and ran into someone in town, she'd received the cold shoulder. If she didn't love her family home so much, she would have left a long time ago. After losing her mother, Liv couldn't bear the thought of letting go of this place.

Ed kicked up a dust storm as he pulled alongside Corbin's truck. Ed opened the door and strode over, tucking a file folder underneath his left arm. The early fifties Realtor was medium height and build, with a thick middle. He wore ironed jeans, a collared shirt with a bolo tie, and a Stetson. He had a ruddy complexion and a hawk-like nose that was too big for his small gray eyes.

"Pleasure seeing you, Mr. Firebrand." Ed stuck out his hand to Corbin, his gaze skipping over Liv.

"How can we help you, Ed?" Corbin took the offering and returned a vigorous-looking shake. He stared down at their hands when Ed didn't let go.

"Oh." Ed withdrew his hand and pulled a white handkerchief from his back pocket, using it to wipe the beads of sweat that had suddenly formed on his forehead. It was late June, and the temperatures weren't nearly as hot as they were about to get. From Fourth of July to as late as the end of September, it would be melt-the-bottom-of-your-flipflops hot. This had been a mild day thanks to the threat of rain that never transpired. Still, Ed started sweating.

Liv wondered whether his sudden bout of nerves had something to do with the fact that Corbin was at her place.

"I drove over to speak to Miss Holden about possibly listing this here property." Ed took off his hat as he acknowledged Liv. Good of him to finally do that, considering he was trying to convince her to allow him to represent her in the sale of her family home.

"This isn't a good time," Liv said. She took note of the fact Corbin didn't step aside.

"Are you sure you don't have a few minutes to hear what I have to say?" Ed's lips compressed, like he was trying to hold something back...anger? He grabbed the folder that he'd tucked underneath one of his arms. "I have all the information and paperwork you need right here and I'm the best man for the job."

Liv didn't even want to get started on the fact that plenty of women Realtors were just as qualified and could do an equally good job. Chauvinism aside, she hadn't actually asked for his services and resented the thought he was ready to shove papers in her face.

"No one else will jump at the chance to work with you," Ed pressed, then waved the folder around. "And I have a surprise in here that another Realtor won't be able to bring to the table."

"An offer?" she asked, not bothering to hide her shock. Although, she shouldn't be surprised someone out there wanted her to move along quickly with a sale.

"Sign the papers to let me represent you and I'm authorized to talk about what comes next," Ed said. With his free hand, he made the gesture of locking his lips and throwing away the key.

"Like I said, this isn't the time. Why don't you give me your folder and I'll look it over?" Liv sidestepped Corbin as Ed tucked the folder underneath his arm and turned away from her.

The move struck her as strange, like a little kid holding onto a toy.

"If I show you my hand, what's to stop you from taking

this to another Realtor?" he asked, like he'd just answered the sixty-four-thousand-dollar question.

Little did he seem to know his pushiness was only serving to push her away.

"I'm sure whoever I choose will do a great job," she stated, slowly, so he didn't miss a word. "And if someone wants to buy this place, they'll be able to go through proper channels."

He opened the file folder wide enough to pull out a business card. Who used those anymore? She took the offering and tucked it inside her back pocket, figuring it was the best way to get rid of him.

"Good to see you, sir." Ed saluted Corbin before smiling at her. "I'll hope to call on you again soon."

"Not if I can help it," she muttered as Ed climbed inside his pickup truck. He backed up, causing another dust cloud. She tapped Corbin on the arm, ignoring how much it felt like poking a brick wall. "You weren't much help."

For the first time in a long time, Corbin smirked.

"Didn't think you needed the assist. You seemed to be handling Ed Roberts just fine," he said with pride she couldn't afford to notice or dwell on. He'd been clear. He wanted no part of her once he got inside his truck and drove away.

"The guy is a jerk and there's no way he'll get my business," she stated matter of fact.

"I understand your position and agree he doesn't deserve your time. In business, and that's what a real estate transaction boils down to, it's best to focus on making the most money. He hinted at having a buyer's name in that file folder. If someone wants this property enough to send Ed a bid before it goes on the market, there might be an offer that's worth investigating," he pointed out.

"Stop making so much sense, dang it." She tapped him on the arm before pulling her hand back like she broke it.

He captured her wrist and caught her gaze. The air between them charged, like a brewing thunderstorm. Corbin let go almost as fast before turning back to the house to avoid the dust cloud shifting their way.

Liv sucked in a burst of clean air before following. Touching Corbin was a bad idea. No more touching. No even thinking about touching. It was dangerous, especially when she looked into those blue eyes of his. His hair was so dark it was almost black. He had the whole chiseled jaw, male model look down pat. It was almost funny to think of him as a cattle rancher. Someone as hot as Corbin belonged on a billboard selling cologne or expensive watches or men's underwear.

Despite being part of one of the wealthiest families in Texas, Corbin was incredibly down to earth. His outfit of boots, jeans, and t-shirt couldn't be any simpler or look any better on a human. She decided walking behind him was a bad idea, so she moved up beside him, stopping at the plastic bag. Poor creature.

"What are you going to do with him?" She motioned toward the bag.

"Take him way out to the back of your property and bury him," he said.

She nodded, wishing there was something they could do to bring the little guy back. "How do you think it happened?"

"Could be poison. Your guess is as good as mine as to how he got into it," he said, putting on a fresh pair of gloves and picking up the bag. "It's possible he was already dead when someone found him. At least, that's what I hope, or we might have a bigger problem brewing in Lone Star Pass."

She'd read an article that said serial killers often started out harming animals as they worked their way up to humans.

"I'll wait out here." A creepy feeling crawled down her spine and she didn't want to go inside without Corbin. Her traitorous heart skipped a few beats looking at him. She couldn't deny the ache losing their friendship had created. She'd never been one to have a dozen friends on the surface. Give her one or two people she could go deep with and...

It didn't matter now.

Looking back, they should have wrecked their friendship in high school by giving in and dating rather than taking the safe route. The one that was supposed to lead to lifelong best buddies. This way, they never got to date *and* they ruined their friendship.

Missed opportunity? *Yes.*

Regret? *Yes.*

Would she go back and change the way she'd handled things when he'd asked her out in high school if she had the chance? That wasn't even a fair question at this point.

Yes. Yes. Yes.

CORBIN STOPPED off at Liv's storage shed on his way to the wooded part of her property. He knew this land well, considering he'd grown up just as much here as at the family ranch. There were so many memories. Good memories. Memories of the two of them spending Saturday nights watching a movie and eating popcorn on the couch. Memories of running through the creek on a hot summer day. Memories of carving their initials just about anywhere they could find a spot. It seemed a shame to sell the place.

That was selfishness talking.

Considering their history—never mind her history with his cousin—and couple that with the amount of electricity buzzing between him and Liv, her moving on was probably for the best in the long run.

The ground near the creek bed would be the softest. He set the bag down and then pushed the shovel into the dirt. A decent burial needed to be two feet deep. He dug three just to be safe. Anger fired through him at the senseless killing. Even more at the fact someone used this poor animal to threaten Liv.

Make no mistake about it, he viewed this as a threat no matter how much he downplayed the incident with Liv.

After tossing his gloves in the hole, covering the plastic bag and tamping down the refilled dirt, Corbin reached for his cell. He pulled up Kellan's name on his contacts. For a long moment, he contemplated making the call and telling Kellan to back off. Would his cousin deny it? Would making the call do more damage than good?

Acting out in the heat of the moment was probably not the right play for Corbin. Kellan was a hothead. Corbin had tamed his own temper years ago when he realized it only served to make matters worse. He couldn't think of one time when losing his cool had actually improved a situation. Give him five minutes with a punching bag and that was a different story. Hell, give him an hour to put in a good workout and he could work off a heckuva lot of his frustration. Sports had saved him from a whole lot of trouble in high school. Now, he was a grown man. And ever since he'd developed hair on his chest, he'd gained control of his outbursts.

On a sharp sigh, he tucked his phone in his back pocket and headed back toward Liv's house. The thought of her being alone after a dead raccoon was dropped on her doorstep caused the hairs on the back of his neck to prick. Had Kellan gone from threatening texts to killing animals? It seemed a stretch, even for a jerk like him. Liv had mentioned others in the community shunning her. How far would they go?

The thought of leaving her vulnerable didn't sit well. Didn't she mention something about an interview in two days? He could get her through forty-eight hours and then be done with her for the rest of his life. Even if he wanted the situation to be different, that was reality. He and Kellan might not be the best of buds, but Corbin wouldn't go behind his cousin's back with his soon-to-be ex-wife, even if she *had* been his friend first. In fact, if Corbin was being honest, he had no idea what Liv saw in Kellan. She was intelligent, fiery, and beautiful. Her mind was sharp. She was the total package.

But Kellan?

Other than pure brute force and family name, Corbin couldn't figure out what Liv had seen in his cousin. All she'd had to do was ask, and Corbin would have told her straight out that she and Kellan wouldn't get along.

Based on comments and not because Corbin cared one way or the other, Kellan was seen as good looking by most. He wasn't stupid either. He lacked a whole lot in the sense of humor department. And the guy was about as intense as they come. He took the whole eldest male in the family a bit too seriously. Hell, he was only six months older than Adam. The two were born in the same year and in the same grade. *Lucky teachers,* Corbin thought wryly, considering Kellan and Adam seemed to go out of their way to frustrate each other.

As Corbin broke free from the tree line, his heart

stopped at the image of Liv standing on the porch, waiting for him. She waved the second he came into view. Based on the way she fiddled with the string on her joggers, he could tell just how high her stress levels were.

She'd made a good point. It couldn't be easy to divorce a Firebrand and stay in Lone Star Pass. He wanted her to be safe. She deserved some peace of mind. Besides, it might be hard to nail an interview if she couldn't sleep for fear the prankster would return with an even bigger threat this time. There was only one way he could think of to ensure someone had her back.

Well, damn. Had he just made the decision to stick around for the next forty-eight hours to make sure she got to her interview okay?

She was making quick work of the casing on the string and she kept shifting her weight from one foot to the other. She was too proud to let him see how vulnerable she was feeling. Corbin bit back a few more of those choice words.

"I'll stay," he said to her with a warning look. "But only because the raccoon didn't deserve his fate and neither did you."

"What does that mean exactly?" Her eyebrows shot up and her forehead wrinkled.

"I want to make sure you get rest between now and your interview. You won't be able to do that if you're checking behind you every two seconds or concerned something else might show up on your porch." There. He'd said it. There was no taking it back now even if he wanted to, which he didn't. He might regret the offer and his family might never let him forget it. Could he take care of Liv and keep it a secret?

"Wow. What can I say? This is...incredible." The fact she was so caught off guard by his kindness showed how unfairly she was used to being treated in Lone Star Pass. More of that anger surfaced because no one deserved to be treated like that. "Thank you, Corbin."

When she caught his gaze, he saw the mix of fear and gratitude and something that looked a whole lot like past regret in her eyes. She crossed the back porch and then held the door open.

Heaven help him, he thought as he walked inside.

"When and where is this interview?" Corbin asked as he reclaimed his coffee mug. He held it up, indicating he needed a refill. Too bad more caffeine couldn't fix stupid—stupid for thinking he could slip under the radar while she was a target.

"Right." She picked up her own mug and started toward the half-full carafe.

"I'll do it." He heard the crankiness in his own voice but didn't bother apologizing. The next day and a half was going to be agony, and he could only hope word didn't get back to Kellan. Considering Ed Roberts had shown up a little while ago, their chance of keeping this a secret dwindled considerably. Maybe Kellan would back off now.

Liv held out her mug and he took it from her without a whole lot of fanfare. It didn't take long to top off both and when he turned around, she was sitting at the table. He might as well take a seat and get some basic details of what she'd been going through so he could get a sense of how he could best help.

"You asked about the interview." She picked up the mug he'd set down and immediately took a sip. "It's on Monday in the middle of the afternoon in Dallas."

"Right. Dallas." He didn't mean to say the word out loud or with such condemnation. He didn't have anything against the city itself so much as the fact it was taking Liv far away.

"I told you that I wouldn't run into anyone from Lone Star Pass in the grocery there. Dallas is a big city and there are millions of people. Just what I need." She said the last part low and almost under her breath.

"That's at least a five-and-a-half-hour drive from here if traffic cooperates and it rarely does," he pointed out.

"If I leave at five a.m., I'll be in Dallas by ten-thirty to eleven if all goes well. I'll have time to eat something and calm my nerves before the interview." Her voice was tinged with defensiveness. She pulled her hair away from her face and held it back with one hand while picking up the pencil with the other. *Tap. Tap. Tap.*

He covered her hand with his, quieting the tapping noise. More of that electricity jolted up his arm but he chose to ignore it. If hiding his true feelings about Liv qualified as a sport, he'd be a professional at this point. In the past, their friendship had made it worth the sacrifice. Now, he didn't have either.

"I'll stay under one condition," he leveled his gaze at her.

"Which is?" She met his stare and held it.

"That's it. We're done. No more contact once you're gone. You can't reach out to me ever again." He removed his hand from hers before she had a chance to do the same.

"Fine," she agreed. Chin up and shoulders back, she dropped the pencil onto the table. "What was I going to do anyway? Call you?" She shook her head. "No, thanks."

Those last two words had an effect on his heart—an effect that was a stark reminder he couldn't let his guard down around Liv.

3

"It's getting dark outside. Since I happen to know you wake before the chickens, I'd like to offer my bathroom to you." Liv tried her best to cover up how hurt she was by Corbin's comment. A light tone. A forced smile. Was he buying it though?

"You can drink coffee and go to sleep after?" His eyebrow shot up.

"Yes. But I'm not the one who goes to bed when the sun goes down, so I'll read for a while," she quipped. Breaking off contact with Corbin would most definitely be for the best. The situation was a no-win. So, why did the thought nearly crush her?

Their shared history was most likely the reason. Losing her mother two years ago without any other relatives she'd been close to had sent her adrift. Had she made decisions back then she regretted? Clearly, the answer to the question was yes. Mistakes were made. Mistakes that couldn't easily be undone. Mistakes that had her closing the door on her hometown forever. A surprising tear sprang to her eye. There was no use beating down that bush. Life threw curveballs at times. She was trying to learn to shift accordingly without beating herself up too much.

"That's fair. I'll grab my overnight bag from the truck." He stood up and walked the couple of steps to the backdoor. He stopped with his hand on the knob, and then turned his head to the side without looking directly at her. "I'll use your bathroom, but just to be clear, I'll be spending the night in my truck."

"Well, I wasn't planning on sleeping together, if that's what you think," she fired back. She couldn't let herself believe it was a mistake to reach out to Corbin, no matter how much it felt like one at the moment. Seeing his contempt for her braided her stomach lining. And yet, there had to be a part of him that remembered old times. If not, he wouldn't have answered her SOS in the first place. He certainly wouldn't have shown up. And he most definitely wouldn't be making plans to stick around to protect her.

Her cell buzzed. She picked it up and checked the screen. *Uncle Jody?*

"Hello?" she answered, not bothering to hide her surprise.

"How are you?" Uncle Jody asked, sounding concerned.

"Okay-y-y." She stretched out the last letter unsure of where he was going with this and why he picked this moment to call. She couldn't remember the last time she'd heard from him. Talk about a blast from the past.

"Do you need anything or..." His voice trailed off.

Right. He used to live in Lone Star Pass. In fact, he grew up here, so he must still have ties.

The back door opened, and Corbin stepped inside. His eyebrow shot up when he saw her on a call.

She shrugged.

"What makes you think I need something?" she asked,

figuring she didn't want to feed any unnecessary information to an uncle she barely spoke to. Plus, this call was so out of the blue she was left scratching her head as to the timing.

"Heard you were going through a rough patch." His answer was about as non-committal as they come.

"I'm good," she reassured, figuring it was time to turn the tables. "How about you? Everything going okay?"

"Yep," he stated, and then said nothing.

The line went quiet for what felt like an eternity but was probably less than a minute. She glanced at the ceiling and then counted the number of dishes on the counter.

"Well, if you need any advice or help with anything..." His voice trailed off once more.

"I'll keep the offer in mind," she reassured.

"I'm glad you brought that up. Have you gotten any offers on your grandmother's old place?" Uncle Jody asked.

"This is my mom's place," she corrected. How on earth would he know to ask a question like that?

Because small towns weren't known for keeping secrets, she thought bitterly. Another reason why a city the size of Dallas appealed to her.

"Sorry, Uncle Jody," she began. "I just realized the time. I'm late, so I should go," she said.

"Oh, well, if you have to," he said, surprise gave him an edge to his tone. "I'd like to come by and pay a visit soon."

"That would be nice," she lied before ending the call. She didn't know the man from Adam but didn't have it in her heart to be rude to the only family she had left.

"Who was that?" Corbin asked casually, looking like he cared more than he was letting on.

"My so-called uncle." She picked up the pencil and started tapping it on the table.

"Jody Reiss? Seemed like a strange conversation to have

with him." Corbin set his backpack down next to the leg of the table.

"The call came out of nowhere," she said. "And he's not technically my uncle."

"Remind me how he's related. Wasn't he somehow connected to your mother?" he asked.

"Yes. I call him uncle out of courtesy but he's my mom's second cousin. He moved away from Lone Star Pass more than a decade ago," she said. "Suddenly, he knows I'm selling this place. It's weird."

"He might have been calling because he found out the divorce is final and wanted to help," he offered. Of course he would say something like that. His family would come together in a time of crisis, whereas all she'd ever had was her mother. And now? There was no one she could count on. More reasons to leave this place behind and start fresh.

"Almost final," she corrected. "I haven't signed the papers to make anything official yet."

Not that she wouldn't once her family home was removed from the equation. She also needed to make sure nothing was hiding in the document. The only reason Kellan would ask for this place was to use a bargaining chip.

"Can I ask why not?" Corbin took a seat and reclaimed his coffee mug. He didn't seem to mind the coffee was cold by now

"I wanted to get a second opinion," she said.

"You need a lawyer?" he asked.

She nodded. And before he hit her up with another question, she said, "No one locally wanted to represent me. In fact, it was hard to find a lawyer in the state willing to take my side against the Firebrand family." She blew out a frustrated breath. "I'm sure everything in the papers is legitimate, but I'd feel better if a real attorney looked over the document before I signed it."

"Who were you able to get?" he continued, his arched eyebrow said he didn't like what he was hearing.

"Haley Smidt." Barely out of law school with virtually no experience in divorce.

Corbin shot her a look.

"I know. She's the only one who would take my case," she defended with a shrug. "I think there's software that will let me scan the legal document in and it'll flag any potential problems. That's pretty much what I'm reduced to at this point, but my first priority has been getting a job so I can move." The small inheritance from her mother was running out and she'd spent the past year in Galveston, finishing up much-needed certification and volunteering in order to pad her resume.

"Maybe you're not ready to sign for other reasons." He didn't make eye contact, but he should be able to feel her reaction for all the anger she sent his way.

"And what would those be since you seem to know me so well?" She couldn't contain the bitterness in her voice. Had she made a mistake in marrying Kellan? *Hell, yes*. Did she need her nose rubbed in it? *No.*

"I have no idea why you would have married him in the first place." Corbin held his hands up, palms out, in the surrender position.

The last thing she wanted to do was explain her reasoning to Kellan's cousin. Allowing herself to believe she could love Kellan was bad enough on her part. He'd made it easy in the beginning, though. He'd been charming and attentive after her mother died. He'd pursued her until she finally gave in and agreed to a date. He gave the impression he'd won the big prize at the county fair when she'd said yes. Now, she couldn't help but wonder if half the reason he'd pursued her so hard was to somehow get back at Corbin.

Being honest with Kellan about her feelings for someone else had been mistake number two. And since bad things usually traveled in threes, she'd agreed to marry him, thinking she would fall in love with him at some point when she stopped loving...

No sense going down that road again.

Once they married, Kellan shifted gears. He became a class-A jerk, demanding she leave the past behind and figure out a way to be happy. And then she realized she'd only ever been a 'prize' in his eyes. Someone to be 'won' instead of loved. Kellan could go beat his chest all day now. He'd done it. She'd married him. Good for him.

She snapped the pencil in two.

CORBIN HADN'T MEANT to set Liv off. He wasn't quite ready to get over being angry with her, but he needed to set aside his feelings for the time being and focus on who was trying to upset her. Plus, the timing of her uncle's call was suspect. Someone seemed to be keeping track of her moves, which meant word could get back about Corbin being at her house.

Maybe it already had?

The last thing Corbin needed was more conflict at home. As it was, his father and his uncle were barely speaking to each other. Ever since Corbin's grandfather died unexpectedly at the beginning of the month, the family had been divided. Divided? Corbin almost laughed out loud. Feuding was probably a better word choice. His father and

Uncle Keifer had always been competitive, driven by the Marshall's need to make them strong, as he'd put it. All he really succeeded in doing was driving a wedge between brothers. A wedge that had turned into a cavern. A cavern there was no bridge long enough to connect sides.

Shame, Corbin thought. With eight brothers and nine cousins, all males, there was enough testosterone at Firebrand Ranch to stir up a few showdowns. But if one of Corbin's brothers needed him, he'd be there without question and vice versa. He didn't think their father could say the same.

"Coffee's gone cold." Liv got up, emptied her mug, and then refilled it.

"Has anyone else crawled out of the woodwork to contact you recently?" Corbin figured he needed to get the conversation back on track.

"No one. It's been quiet until I ran into Ed's wife at the store last month," she said. "He's annoying, but also I think there's so little business in Lone Star Pass that I think he's kind of desperate."

Corbin wasn't so sure. Since it didn't seem like there was much more to discuss for now, he grabbed the handle of his bag. "I'll take you up on that shower now."

The upstairs bathroom was in the middle of two bedrooms. One had been converted into an office and the other, he assumed, was the master. Seeing her personal belongings where she slept when she was home wouldn't help in the least. Staying focused became his new marching orders. So, Corbin kept his head down and walked straight into the bathroom.

He showered military style, which basically meant in and out with a steady stream of cold water. And then he was done, drying off and trying to figure out how he'd signed himself up for this particular brand of torture. And yet the thought of losing Liv forever after this sat hard in his gut. He threw on a fresh outfit, not minding the fact he was going to sleep in jeans and a t-shirt as long as they were clean.

Corbin walked downstairs to find Liv slumped over the kitchen table, head on her arms, asleep. This wasn't the time to get inside his head about the emotions trying to pull him under and wash him out.

Quietly, so as not to wake her, he cut off the kitchen light and then picked her up. She leaned into him, wrapping her arms around his neck. He ignored the way his pulse pounded and electricity vibrated through his body just from holding her. This seemed like a good time to remind himself that he had no designs on her and vice versa.

But, man, she felt right in his arms. It was a fact that refused to be ignored.

Rather than tempt fate and take her to her bedroom, he decided to divert to the sofa in the adjacent living room. He gently set her down, but she immediately protested, holding on tighter to his neck.

In her sleepy state, she murmured his name and his heart clenched. How easy would it be in the moment to go with his feelings and plant a kiss on those cherry lips of hers? Capture the dimple on her chin and feather kisses down her neck?

His feelings had gotten out of control for her once and she'd been smart enough to rein them in, placing the friendship over a temporary physical attraction. It had seemed like the right move at the time. Now? He had regrets.

Yes, they'd preserved their friendship for years. Then, he'd gone on to date Dani Sheldon. They'd stayed together for long after the relationship had played out, then she'd backed him into a corner. Marry her or lose her, those were the choices. She hinted at being pregnant and he'd believed she didn't want him to ask her to marry him solely based on a child coming into the world.

Corbin had taken the hint and bought the ring. He'd gotten down on one knee, knowing full well he wasn't ready. He'd asked the big question, figuring he would get his mind around marriage and fatherhood.

Dani had agreed to marry him. She'd started planning a huge wedding with three hundred guests and twelve bridesmaids. Twelve? Who had that many close friends? Apparently, Dani did. Not even Corbin with his eight brothers and nine cousins had twelve guys he considered close enough to him to be in his wedding party. When he'd asked Dani if they could tone down the wedding, she'd burst into tears, crying that they didn't want the same things in life.

He couldn't have agreed more. He'd told her that they would need to learn to compromise, especially when their kid came into the world. Her tears had turned to laughter. *A kid?* she'd said. Then, she'd come clean. There was no pregnancy. She'd only mentioned the possibility so he'd decid if he was in or out of the relationship.

It was that moment he realized he'd made a huge mistake. Undoing the whole affair took a few more weeks. By then, Liv had run off to Vegas and married Kellan. Talk about strange circumstances and twists of fate. He never would have believed any of it if it hadn't happened to him. The whole incident had been surreal and not something he wanted to repeat anytime soon.

The worst part was that Liv's mother had died a few months before and he wondered if he'd made it clear to Liv how sorry he was and how much he missed Ms. Holden. She'd been his favorite teacher sophomore year of high school, and she'd probably gone too easy on him. Knowing her personally and being best friends with her daughter had probably given her blinders toward him. He was smart and pulled good grades on his own merit. But still.

The memories caused a rush of nostalgia and it suddenly felt like his chest was caving in. This was the first time he'd allowed himself to think about Ms. Holden since her death two years ago.

Looking down at Liv now, he couldn't help but feel like an overwhelming failure. She rolled onto her side and his heart took a serious hit. He pulled the blanket that was draped over the back of the sofa over her to keep her warm. A/C in Texas was nothing to be joked about, most folks set the temperature low enough to need thick covers at night and she'd kept hers on.

Corbin took great care in placing a pillow underneath Liv's head. He situated the covers to make certain she was comfortable. At this point, he couldn't help but wonder how little sleep she'd been getting. Between the threatening texts, which still made his muscles tense up thinking about them, the tires, and now the raccoon, he wondered how well she'd been resting, if at all.

Anger heated the blood in his veins past the boiling point. She didn't deserve to be treated like this. No one did. Liv wasn't the type to take getting a divorce lightly. She would see it as a failure, and it would bother her for the rest of her life. Her heart was built that way. Even though she was being tight-lipped about the cause, Corbin was certain she had her reasons. Had she been drowning in sorrow after losing her mother? She'd refused to talk to him about it, telling him he needed to spend more time with his fiancée. Those words had stung at the time and weren't much better when he thought about them now. She'd pushed him away and he couldn't figure out why.

Again, she wasn't the type to take marriage for granted. So, the question remained, what had Kellan done?

Could Corbin go to his cousin and confront him? That was almost laughable, he thought. Kellan was as likely to take his part of the blame as cold weather was to come in June. Just thinking about the texts his cousin had sent caused the muscle in Corbin's jaw to tick.

He stared down at Liv, fisting his hands to keep them from reaching out to touch her. Even though they'd lost touch in the past eighteen months, he realized how much he was going to miss her. Moving away to Dallas felt so final.

The knot in Corbin's stomach tightened as he thought about losing her forever despite realizing it was most likely for the best for both of them.

Well, that wasn't exactly true. The optimal scenario had her sticking around and the two of them hanging around each other like old times. Best friends, two people who could share everything without fear of judgment. Thinking about what might have been literally threatened to rip his heart out of his chest. Too late now.

Shame, he thought.

4

A noise startled Liv awake. She bolted upright and desperately tried to get her bearings.

"You're okay," Corbin's deep baritone soothed. His voice had a habit of washing over her and through her in the most inconvenient way.

She blinked a couple of times to make sure he wasn't a mirage as he walked toward her. And then he was next to her, kneeling beside the sofa.

"I must have fallen asleep," she said, fixing the cover that had fallen off as she sat up.

"When I got out of the shower, I found you head-down at the kitchen table," he admitted, his tone so much less angry at her than before. What caused the change?

"Oh." She bit back a yawn. "Strange. But I guess I haven't really slept in a few weeks. Longer than that if I'm honest."

"Is that because of the divorce?" he asked.

"That, plus knowing I was coming back here where, for at least two seconds, I thought I might stay." She took in a deep breath and nodded. "But enough is enough. I give. Time to pack up and move on."

"You've always been braver than you realized and more bullheaded than an ox." Was he complimenting her?

She must be losing it or still asleep because when she looked into his eyes, she saw compassion and another emotion she couldn't quite pinpoint that had been missing all day.

"What time is it?" she asked. "And why are you still awake?"

"Nine o'clock," he stated after checking his cell phone. "I have no plans to sleep tonight."

"You must be starving." Her stomach reminded her that she hadn't eaten dinner and the couple cups of coffee she polished off were now making her nauseous.

"I have a power bar in my overnight bag. It's usually enough to get me through," he said, and she realized why. He went out sometimes for days on end tracking dangerous poachers. His body was trained to get very little sleep and need only enough food to sustain his energy.

"I can do better than that," she said, throwing the cover off.

Corbin offered a hand up, and a jolt of electricity vibrated through her hand and up her arm at contact. The two stood in her living room, not two feet apart. Their gazes locked and something pinged in the space between them, charging the air with electrical impulses. Suddenly, her throat dried up and she couldn't find words.

Liv's thoughts scrambled as a fog rolled in—the fog that was Corbin Firebrand. This close, his spicy male scent consumed her senses and her fingers itched to reach out and touch him. *Really* touch him.

And just to make certain she didn't make another mistake with Corbin, she shoved her hands inside the pockets of her hoodie. She swallowed, trying to ease some of the dryness in her throat and broke eye contact.

"I made those sour cream chicken enchiladas you like so much," she croaked out. "The ones my grandmother used to make."

He took in a deep breath and an emotion stirred behind his eyes that she couldn't quite pinpoint. He must have noticed she'd skipped over the fact her mother used to make the dish from her granny's recipe.

"Sounds good." Those two words spoken through clenched teeth told her that he was struggling too.

Since she didn't want to make this any more difficult for him and she could see that she was, she said, "I loved him in my own way."

Her words looked like the equivalent of a bucket of ice water being thrown in Corbin's face, just as she knew they would, shocking him back to reality.

"Yeah? Good." Two words sentences weren't a good sign despite the fact he'd used the word twice.

At least his cold shoulder returned, giving her the bravado to walk into the kitchen and away from him. It was a low blow to say those words to him about Kellan, but they were true. She had loved him in a way. Turned out not to be the kind of caring that could go the distance but he'd been a saving grace when her heart had been shattered...first by Corbin and then her mother.

Liv shook off the memory. That was a long time ago and a lot had changed. Corbin no longer had the power to rip her heart out of her chest. No one had that kind of influence over her. He was simply stepping in as a good person willing to help a fellow friend in need. Her mother was gone and there was no bringing her back, so it was time to accept the reality, sell the house, and move on.

She pulled the enchiladas out of the fridge and split the leftovers onto two plates. A minute later, a ding from the microwave, and dinner was ready. She set the plates down and moved to the entryway.

Corbin sat on the edge of the sofa, head in his hands. She would ask if everything was okay, but she realized he was between a rock and hard place.

"Dinner's on the table," she said softly, wishing she'd found another way to put up a wall between them rather than bringing up his cousin.

He looked up and seemed to think long and hard about his next words.

"I don't mind giving up the weekend to help you out. You'll be gone soon, out of this town and my life forever. After what happened, it seems like you need a real friend," he started and her heart dropped at hearing the pain in his voice. "But if you bring up your relationship with my cousin again…I'm out. Understand?"

When he caught her gaze, she saw a mix of anger and what looked a whole lot like regret. Her heart felt like it had been ripped out of her chest. Since trying to go back in the past to change something was as productive as trying to milk a bluebonnet, she forced the thought aside.

"Okay." She received his message loud and clear. No more talk about Kellan. The awkward silence that followed had her wanting to blurt out almost anything to fill the air. After a few moments and with no wisdom to make this better, she finally said, "Food's getting cold."

"Go ahead and start without me. I'll be right in." Again, the hurt in his voice was a knife stab to the center of her chest.

There was no reason for him to let her know that he was in pain now. He'd asked Dani to marry him, and Dani had made her expectations clear to Liv. Their friendship might be okay before the wedding, but Liv was to steer clear of Corbin once he was married. Under no terms was Liv to contact Corbin again. Liv could handle Dani, but violate her demand and she would take it out on Corbin. If Dani was the woman he loved, the one he chose to be with, Liv wouldn't stand in the way of their relationship. She cared too much for Corbin to do that. Plus, there was the simple fact she realized she didn't *want* to see him committed to someone else.

Her mind immediately snapped to that lonely place where she'd been distraught beyond measure. Alone. Lonely. She'd done the next best thing to being with Corbin. She'd become a Firebrand. Dani couldn't force Liv away from Corbin once they were technically related. But accepting Kellan's proposal hadn't been out of spite or to circumvent Dani in any way. Liv had been broken after finding out Corbin had proposed to Dani and then her mother had been in the crash on the highway.

There wasn't much she could have done about her mother, but she should have seen Corbin's engagement coming. Yet it had blindsided her in the worst possible way. She'd felt betrayed and all kinds of other feelings that didn't belong in the context of best friends. A line had been crossed by her that they'd sworn never to step over. Corbin had held up his end of the bargain. She'd been the one to fail miserably.

Looking back, being around Kellan had made her feel like she'd come home in an odd way. Hindsight caused her to realize how messed up her thinking had become. Grief had her making bad choices. And now it was too late to undo any of it.

Corbin would always be out of reach with not so much as a friendship between them now. She'd bet and lost big time. And it was probably time to accept it no matter how much her heart protested. The two of them weren't meant to be. Not even friends.

As reality set in, a reality she'd been denying far too long now, she slumped in her seat at the table, picked up her fork, and pushed food around on her plate.

A few minutes later, Corbin joined her. He sat down without making eye contact, picked up his own fork, and stabbed it into his enchilada.

What had she expected? A joyful reunion? Him to tell her how much he'd missed her and that they needed to figure out a way to keep their friendship alive.

Liv almost laughed out loud.

She didn't bother to look at him while they ate. Exhaustion made picking up her fork feel like a herculean effort. The catnap hadn't even made a dent in how tired she was. If she wanted to make a good impression in her interview, she needed to get plenty of rest between now and Monday.

The meal might smell good and she might be hungry but all she managed to do was take enough bites to stop her stomach from growling.

"I overstepped my bounds in asking for your help, Corbin. But I do appreciate the fact that you came, and all that you're doing for me. I realize I've put you in a no-win situation," she admitted, softening her tone.

When he didn't respond, she stood up, walked over to the trash, and emptied her plate. After a quick rinse, she loaded the dishwasher. "Key is on the counter. Lock up when you leave."

Without another word, she left the kitchen and headed

upstairs. Her chin quivered and tears threatened, but she refused to cry. It wouldn't do any good and she'd already shed enough tears over Corbin. This was exactly the closure she needed to move on, no matter how much her heart protested.

THERE WERE SO many words that came to mind as Liv walked out of the kitchen. But Corbin couldn't form a sentence. A mix of anger and regret jumbled his thoughts, and he realized it would be better if he kept his mouth shut. The last thing he wanted to do was add to the tension between him and Liv.

He would follow through on his promise to get her to her interview safely on Monday, and then he would go home. So, why did his heart feel like it was being ripped out of his chest as he emptied his plate and set it in the sink?

He grabbed his toothbrush and toothpaste out of his backpack, and then headed to the hall bath. After brushing his teeth, he located the key, locked up, and headed to his truck where he planned to sleep.

In the backseat, he kept a small pillow and blanket. There were other supplies too. Enough food to keep him from starving if he needed to be gone for a couple of days without warning. Enough water to ensure he didn't dehydrate. And enough camping supplies to keep out the cold or much of the heat depending on the time of year. He wouldn't need much more than a pillow tonight.

After leaning the seat back, Corbin rolled the windows down. In late June, the nights were still cool enough for him to be comfortable inside the vehicle. Tonight was no exception. The temperature was supposed to drop into the mid-sixties. They hadn't yet reached the time of year when he would wake to eighty-plus degrees and go to sleep to more than a hundred. It was coming, though. Soon enough. The drought threatened to dry up what little grass was left, and the cattle would have to be moved north if that happened.

As troubling as those facts were, the unsettled feeling that had been hovering over Corbin since his grandfather had died earlier in the month had intensified over the course of the evening. Something was off here. Something was bugging him, niggling at the back of his mind. If only he could put his finger on what it was.

Looking out the front windshield at the expansive sky that seemed to go on forever, Corbin tried to shut off his thoughts. He'd noticed a long time ago that concentrating on a problem only served to make it worse. The best way to find an answer was to distract himself. Shutting off his racing thoughts, however, was a whole other story. Counting sheep never worked. Neither did putting on music or ambient noise. He'd tried breathing techniques.

At some point in the night, although he couldn't pinpoint when, he finally closed his eyes.

CORBIN RUBBED his eyes and sat up. He squinted. His mouth was dry and his tongue had a sweet taste. His brain was foggy. How long had he been out? He'd gone days without sleep and not felt this out of it. What was different this time?

Moving his arms took more effort than if he'd dragged them through a lake filled with molasses. Something was off, mentally and physically. He tried to shake off the fog gripping him like octopus tentacles pulling him down to the ocean floor.

He needed to get his bearings. The sun was rising to his left against the eastern horizon.

In this out-of-body state, it took a couple of seconds for him to realize the farmhouse was on fire. Smoke billowed from the back of the house. He muttered a curse and reached for his cell as he jammed his shoulder into the door, pulling on the latch with his free hand.

The situation snapped his mind into focus. The average older home took roughly fifteen minutes to burn, newer ones took a third of the time due to being made of mostly synthetic materials. There was no way he could wait for a volunteer firefighter to arrive. That could take half an hour or longer in these parts and there would be nothing left of the house, let alone Liv.

It had to be a good sign he was catching this early since he saw only smoke and no flames, he thought as he bolted around the back of the house where her bedroom was located.

Corbin managed to hit 911 on his cell as he shouted up at Liv's window. There was no response. He circled the building looking for the best entry point. Make no mistake about it, he was going inside.

"Nine-one-one, what's your emergency?" Georgia Vincent's voice came on the line. She'd been widowed for half a decade, days after her fiftieth birthday.

"This is Corbin Firebrand. I'm at Liv Holden's residence and her home is on fire. There's no time to explain. Send help. I'm going in." He dropped the phone onto a patch of dried grass to keep it from overheating inside the house.

There was more smoke in back, so he determined the front would be the best angle. He fumbled for the key in his pocket, and then tested the door handle for heat. It was fine, so he unlocked the door. The lack of heat registered as odd.

"Liv," he shouted. Still no response but the smoke was so thick he couldn't see across the room as he entered. Don't even get him started on how the place could have been set on fire without him realizing while he was parked next to the building. After two steps inside, he choked and gagged. His eyes burned and it felt like someone had set his nose on fire. Burnt wood stuck in the back of his throat.

Corbin pulled his t-shirt up over his nose and barreled into the house, expecting to see flames and be hit with a wave of heat unlike anything he'd ever experienced. He cut an immediate right and raced up the stairs, taking two at a time.

Given the amount of smoke, he figured he didn't have a whole lot of time before the place went up in flames. He stopped halfway up the stairs, realizing how thick the smoke had become. He coughed, chugging air. His throat burned. His chest felt like it was on fire. And still no flames or heat.

"Liv," he shouted before gagging as he crested the stairs. Shouldn't alarms be going off at her house at this point? Corbin made a mental note of the issue and moved on. There was no time to analyze her fire readiness. Besides, who thought there would ever be a blaze inside her home to begin with?

She must've have heard him this time because the silhouette of her feminine frame filled the doorway. Coughing, she had something wrapped around her nose and mouth as she made a run toward him. He caught her with one arm, and they bolted down the stairs and out the front door, fingers linked.

"There's a hose in front and back," she managed to say through coughs.

"I'll take the back." He figured he might get a clue as to how a fire could have started in the first place.

Again, something felt off, but he couldn't put his finger on it. And then it dawned on him. There were still no flames. Was there even a fire to put out?

5

Granted, there was enough smoke to fill four corn silos, and then some. What was the source? Corbin didn't see flames shooting out the windows, which they would be by now. And shouldn't it be burning hot?

Liv was already on the hose in front, opening the valve and spraying water as he bolted around back and located its twin. He hit the house with a steady spray from the backside.

Sirens split the air and all he could think was how this could have started? Or *who* had done it? Pranks were one thing. The dead raccoon had been a warning. The fire, or whatever this turned out to be, was personal.

Was there any way Kellan could be behind this? Despite their differences of opinion, and there was no shortage there, Corbin had a hard time believing his cousin would be capable of criminal activity. The last time he'd checked, being a jerk wasn't illegal.

Studying the back of the house as his eyes adjusted to the dark, Corbin realized a kitchen window had been broken. How had he missed it before? It was the same kind of break as when a baseball was accidentally tossed too far in the wrong direction. Could someone have thrown a Molotov cocktail?

A marked SUV roared up to the scene. Less than a minute later, Sheriff Timothy Lawler rounded the corner of the house. He had a fire extinguisher in hand as he joined the fight. Lawler had been two grades ahead of Corbin's older brother Adam in school, so those two knew of each other. Corbin, however, had been too young. All he knew about Lawler was that he'd been a star quarterback at one time who was being scouted by some big-name programs. He took a hit senior year that broke his arm in several places, four to be exact. Still, he'd managed to get off the game-winning throw, but the injury had ended his career and any hopes of playing college ball.

Lawler healed, rehabbed, and then went to school to study criminal justice. He then followed in his father's footsteps in law enforcement. Lawler was about as fair-skinned as they came. He had ginger hair in a military cut. He also had a hawk-like nose and compassionate light-brown eyes. He wore jeans, boots, and a tan shirt with the word, *Sheriff*, embroidered on the right front pocket.

"I can't find the source and the window is broken." Corbin pointed as Lawler joined him. Keeping his presence at Liv's house a secret was no longer going to be an option. A report would be filed, and Kellan would be brought in for questioning. There was no doubt about it after he'd sent those threatening texts. His cousin would be a prime suspect.

Lawler nodded, approaching the building with caution.

"Here's a key." Corbin tossed it to the sheriff, who caught it on the first try. He put the key in the lock, and then tested the door handle, much like Corbin had done in front. Lawler twisted the door handle.

Corbin bit back a string of curses as a fire truck joined in the fray. A pair of volunteer firefighters approached, and Corbin motioned toward Lawler. The pair joined the sheriff. Corbin set down the hose and made a beeline for Liv on the other side of the house.

"How could he?" She sat down on the parched earth, staring at the farmhouse.

"This might be hard to believe coming from me, but I can't imagine Kellan would do anything this cruel," Corbin said.

"I don't want to think so either, and yet my home was on fire nonetheless," she said. "And I can't think of who else would do something so...horrible."

"You were about the sign the papers. Kellan must realize this wouldn't help finalize the matter." He knew in his heart of hearts his cousin wouldn't be this reckless. But he couldn't offer up any other name, so he clamped his mouth closed.

She blinked up at him. "I thought you were on my side on this one, Corbin. What else is it going to take for you to believe that Kellan wants me far away from town?"

"There might not be a fire inside," he stated.

She shot him a look like he had two foreheads.

"I didn't feel any heat inside the house, did you?" he asked, his thought process gaining steam.

She looked up and to the left, a sign of concentration and attempt at recall.

"As a matter of fact, no. What does that prove?" she asked.

"When there's smoke, there isn't always fire," he stated,

motioning toward the house before retrieving his cell phone and slipping it inside his back pocket.

Lawler came from around back. He had a mask on and gloves. He was holding a type of device or can in his right hand as he approached. With his free hand, he raised the mask until they could see all of his face.

"Found this inside the kitchen on the floor," he said, holding out the can on the flat of his palm.

Corbin took a couple of steps to get a closer look. The device's label read: Instafog.

"Are you kidding me?" Corbin said low and under his breath. He looked to Liv, who'd moved beside him. "This all came from a can?"

"With the amount of smoke in the building, I imagine there are others," Lawler said. "We can open doors and windows to let out much of the smoke to investigate."

"I have a few fans that might help move air. Thank heavens it wasn't an actual fire," Liv stated. Wide gaze, compressed lips, she seemed like she was still in a state of shock.

"There's no major damage that we've found so far. A couple of firemen are investigating further since they have the right kind of equipment to survive inside for more than a few seconds," Lawler stated. "Looks as though the smell of smoke will hang around long after we're gone."

She nodded.

"There haven't been any other cases like this one in the area," Lawler said, looking to Liv. "I'd like to ask a few questions if you don't mind."

Normally, Corbin's mind would snap to bored teenagers. Except there was the raccoon yesterday before sundown. Kellan's temper was about to get him into trouble, or at least hauled in for questioning. A question burned... How did the jerk who did this get past him?

"Okay, ask me anything," Liv said on a sigh. "Mind if we find a place to sit down though?"

"Would you like water as well?" Lawler asked after agreeing to find a spot.

"Oh, hold on," she said, snapping her fingers. "I can run inside the kitchen and grab something to drink."

"I'd like a chance to dust the door handles for prints first, if you don't mind." Lawler's statement seemed to catch her off guard based on the face she made.

And then it seemed to click.

"Of course," she said, placing her balled fists on her hips. "Do whatever you need to."

"I've already lifted a print on the can. I'm admitting it into evidence. I'll circle back to take your statement as soon as I finish. I'd like to try to capture prints while the scene is still fresh. Okay?" Lawler asked.

"Yes, of course," she responded. There was a hollow quality to her voice that caused Corbin to think she might be in a state of shock.

Lawler disappeared around the back of the house as Liv turned her full attention on Corbin.

"Still think your cousin is innocent?" Her eyes issued a challenge. He'd seen that look before and it was a no-win situation for him.

As he clamped his mouth shut for the second time, the sound of a vehicle heading toward them on the drive caught his attention.

~

LIV HAD to walk off her frustration. It was either that or scream at the top of her lungs. The sound of a vehicle coming stopped her in her tracks. Instinctively, she reached for Corbin's arm, something to anchor her. Her fingers tingled with electrical impulses the second she made contact, the current so strong she almost jerked her hand back.

Did he feel it too? *Did it matter if he did?*

Pushing the questions aside, her face twisted up when she saw whose truck was barreling toward them. Ed?

Again, Corbin stepped in front of her, effectively blocking her from the older Realtor.

"What in hell is he doing here?" Corbin said in a low growl.

Ed parked away from the activity. He pulled out a jug of what looked like drinking water and walked straight up to her and Corbin.

"Came as fast as I heard," he said with a look of concern that would rival any parent. "Brought water in case you needed it."

"Looks like a smoke bomb went off, nothing more," Corbin put his hand up to stop Ed from coming any closer.

Ed froze, then set the jug down.

"Where did you hear about this?" Liv asked, not bothering to hide her shock. Word couldn't have possibly gotten out despite this being a small town where folks generally cared about their neighbors. Of course, after what Liv had been through recently, she would argue Lone Star Pass had become anything but neighborly.

"I have one of those police radios at the house," he said, sheepishly. "It's a good way to stay in touch if anything happens to one of my listings."

First of all, she had to fight the urge to tell him *this* place wasn't one of his listings and at this point never would be.

"That's not the case here, Ed," she stated.

"Well, now, don't go making any decisions while you're in the heat of the moment," Ed warned. There was an undercurrent in his voice that made the hairs on the back of her neck prick.

"I appreciate your concern," she said, "and thank you for your kindness with the water but there's no reason for you to be here."

"It's what neighbors do," he said dismissively.

"Drive up to an active crime scene? That's what busybodies do." There. She said it. She couldn't help herself.

Ed's mouth dropped open but he didn't respond.

Liv appreciated the fact Corbin didn't butt into the conversation. He seemed content to stand back and watch her handle Ed. She was fully capable of taking care of this guy and anyone else for that matter. This seemed like a good time to remind herself of the fact. She would force him off her property in a heartbeat except that she wanted to figure out his real reasoning for showing up. It couldn't be the listing, could it?

"You didn't have to, so thanks." She stared at him.

"I have the folder in my truck if you'd like to be rid of this place," Ed said when he regained his composure.

Liv shot a look toward Corbin. She could use a little reinforcement since she didn't seem to be getting through.

Corbin took a threatening step forward and Ed instinctively backed away. Time for courtesy was over. "And now that you've dropped it off, you can head home. It's early and—"

"How much damage did the sheriff say the house took?" Ed cut in.

Corbin took in a deliberate, slow breath, like he was making sure Ed knew he was trying Corbin's patience.

Liv needed a breath trick like that because Ed took another entire step back. But then coming in a six-feet-five-inches of stacked muscle, Corbin could be physically intimidating if he wanted to be. And he seemed like he wanted to be with Ed.

Again, Corbin kept silent.

"It's not a big deal," she waved him off.

"My client might want to reconsider his offer," Ed stated.

"The funny thing about your client's offer is that the place isn't even for sale yet." Liv folded her arms across her chest. "Plus, I have no idea who you represent. So, if you have an interested party, you might as well come forward because all this hinting around makes me want to donate the house to charity before I sell it to anyone you represent.."

"This isn't the time for digging heels in and being stubborn," Ed warned.

"Really?" Corbin interjected. "I hope you will stick around because I'm sure the sheriff will need the name of your 'client' for the report."

Blood drained from Ed's face. His mouth fell slack. All the bravado dissipated as fast as the smoke. He backed away another couple of steps before giving Corbin one hell of an evil eye.

"Like I said, I'm just being neighborly. Making sure you have everything you need," Ed stated, taking a couple more steps backward without turning away. He put his hands up like he was backing away from a wild animal.

Corbin could be fierce. She'd seen him take on a bully and his friend who were two grades ahead because they tripped Desi Combs. Desi and Corbin weren't even friends when he'd intervened. It was just his nature to step in when someone else was trying to put on a show of strength or hurt someone or something smaller than them.

"I-uh-the wife will be waiting around for me. Told her that I'd be back before she had time to scramble eggs," Ed said, his gaze darted everywhere but at them.

Sheriff Lawler came from around the back of the house. His gaze flew straight to Ed.

"Sheriff, you know Ed Roberts," Corbin said.

"Followed the smoke," Ed stated, waving his hand in the air, which was not at all what he'd said when he first arrived. Was he lying or shaken up by Corbin's statement about Ed's client being in the report?

"There's nothing to see here," Sheriff Lawler said. "Unless you have something to contribute that I don't know about."

"Ed here claims to have a client interested in buying Liv's home," Corbin continued.

"I didn't realize it was on the market." One of Lawler's eyebrows shot up.

"That's the funny part," Liv said. "It isn't."

"Miss Holden ran into my wife in the supermarket a few weeks ago and mentioned she was considering a move in passing," Ed said by way of defense. "A good salesman gets in early with an aggressive offer that can't be refused." He shrugged. "Plus, you know me, Sheriff. I do what I can to help folks." He dropped his gaze to the jug of water.

"Same can be said for an ambulance chaser," Corbin muttered low and under his breath. So low, in fact, Liv barely heard him. She was certain the comment got past the sheriff and Ed.

"How about you swing by my office in an hour after you've had time to eat breakfast with MaryAnne and we can talk about the client of yours," the sheriff said. "And the real reason you're infringing on a crime scene."

Liv could have sworn she saw Ed break into another sweat.

"Sure thing, Sheriff." Ed saluted and back-peddled. The man couldn't seem to get out of there fast enough.

A pair of firemen rounded the house. One of them called to the sheriff.

"Excuse me for a minute," he said before walking away.

"You do realize that I'm going to be forced to tell Lawler about Kellan's threatening texts now," Liv said, trepidation filled her.

"I know." Based on his tone, he knew how bad this whole scene was going to go down with Kellan.

"It wasn't my intention to bring his name into this," Liv said by way of defense.

"I know that too." Corbin's tone was solemn. Resigned? His family was news and this wasn't going to look good for them. A few buzzards had probably started circling since the Marshall's death. If other ranching operations saw them as weak, it could kick up a whole different storm.

Other news was bound to get out now too. Corbin's presence at her place overnight would definitely raise a few eyebrows. If she hadn't been popular in town before she sure wasn't going to win any awards now. She hadn't thought about the consequences she'd face if word got out when she'd texted him to come over in the first place. Had she just made a bad situation worse?

Liv issued a sharp sigh. She couldn't go there. She couldn't allow herself to think that reaching out to Corbin was wrong. He was her only friend in Lone Star Pass, and tonight had proved she needed him around.

But she hated the wedge this would drive in between

him and Kellan. No one was supposed to know about her plea for Corbin's help. She bit back a curse, thinking how much more complicated this situation had become in a matter of minutes.

A black truck came barreling up the drive. This time, it wouldn't be Ed. She knew exactly who the driver was...Kellan.

6

Kellan's dual cab black pickup kicked up one helluva dust storm as he came barreling toward them, his gaze intent on one thing...Corbin. His cousin needed a reality check if he thought Corbin planned to back down. He dropped his hands to his sides, ready and able to defend himself.

Liv's gaze widened. Out of the corner of his eye, he saw Lawler heading toward them as Kellan exited his truck and made a beeline for Corbin. His cousin stopped when they were nose-to-nose.

"What are you doing here?" Anger vibrated from Kellan's equally tall frame. When it came to height, the two were eye to eye. When it came to tempers, Corbin had reined his in long ago, which didn't mean he would back down to a bully.

"Helping a friend," Corbin responded with the kind of calm demeanor that came with years of experience of holding his temper in check.

"Last I checked, your 'friend' was my wife. That makes

this my business." Kellan barely got the words out before Liv shoved him back a step.

Kellan immediately stepped forward, determined not to lose any ground, and puffed out his chest. The hurt in his eyes struck Corbin square in the chest. Hurt that Kellan was doing his level best to cover with anger.

Corbin studied his cousin, searching for any signs of guilt over his actions. Those texts should make him feel like a real jerk.

"Calm down or we'll have to take this conversation to my office," Lawler said. He wedged a hand in between the two of them, but Kellan refused to ease up.

Corbin had no plans to back down. He was well within his rights to be there.

"You have a problem with me?" Corbin asked. "We can handle this back at the ranch or right here. Your choice."

The best way to diffuse a bully was to stand his ground. Corbin had learned the lesson a long time ago. To be fair, once he filled out his tall frame no one came at him. Prior, though, he'd taken his fair share of snide remarks, elbow jabs, and threatening looks.

Lawler strong-armed Kellan, who seemed to think twice about throwing a punch at or in front of an officer of the law.

Loyalty and family weren't words Corbin took lightly. There were others too. Friendship being one of them, despite the fact he and Liv had gone their separate ways. But then, they would probably still be close if circumstances hadn't pushed them apart. Her mother's death had been hard on her. Corbin's relationship with Dani had heated up. And then it looked like Liv had developed serious feelings for Kellan, feelings Corbin questioned now. Would Liv had gotten into a relationship with Kellan if Dani hadn't played the pregnancy card?

Then, Liv had cold-shouldered him almost immediately after his engagement and he still didn't fully understand why. He'd been naïve, an annoying voice in the back of his mind pointed out. He'd believed he could marry Dani and still keep his best friend by his side. Once he realized the person he'd truly fallen for was Liv, she'd gone and married his cousin before he could intervene. And, yes, he did realize he never answered her question from earlier about why he didn't go through with the marriage to Dani. There was no way he could tell her the real reason and he didn't have it in him to make up a lame excuse.

Life became too complicated to untangle once Liv came home from Vegas a married woman. He'd been trying to move on ever since. Except how was he supposed to do that when missing Liv was the equivalent of having his heart ripped from his chest?

And now? Complicated didn't begin to describe their situation.

Corbin didn't break eye contact while he waited for Kellan's response. The death stare routine wasn't working, but this didn't seem like the right time to point out that fact. Then, there was the fact Liv and Corbin had been best friends long before Kellan had ever asked her out. Plus, the two were getting a divorce. The territorial routine didn't cut it.

Kellan ground his back teeth and it looked like it was taking every ounce of strength not to throw a punch. "Why are you doing this?"

Corbin didn't respond.

"Are you jealous about mineral rights? About the

money? Is this a sick way of getting back at the 'other' side of the family?" Kellan ground out.

"First of all, are you serious? And second, I'm not discussing personal family business here. There's no point airing dirty laundry in public," Corbin said with as calm a voice as he could muster. Besides, he was still weighing all the facts of the inheritance that had drawn sides and further divided their family. "Lastly, Liv and I go back to the third grade. We've been friends a long time and I'm not abandoning her right now when she needs me, and you of all people should know why. Are we clear?"

Kellan issued a sharp sigh, but gave no other reaction. Shouldn't he be ready to defend his actions with the texts?

"This isn't over, Corbin," Kellan said.

"Didn't think it was," Corbin shot back.

Liv stood back and he could feel her seething. She seemed to know speaking up would only make Kellan angrier.

"Why don't you head on home, Kellan?" Lawler suggested, taking a step forward.

"Good idea, Timothy." Kellan was pushing his luck with Lawler. No one called the sheriff by his first name. The two weren't in the same grade so there was no reason for the familiarity.

Lawler didn't bite. He stood his ground until Kellan retreated to his vehicle. The dust cloud he kicked up on the way out had them all moving away from the drive.

"Jerk," Liv mumbled at the same time Corbin thought it.

Turning toward the house, Corbin saw something next to the driver's side of his truck. He ate up the real estate in quick strides. There was a white cloth like a handkerchief.

"What are you looking at over there?" Lawler followed

when he seemed to realize Corbin might have just found a piece of evidence.

"Might be nothing," he said as Liv joined them. He didn't dare touch the cloth just in case.

Lawler picked up a stick and lifted up the cloth with it. There was a distinct smell, and it jogged a memory.

"First of all, I'm a light sleeper so the fact someone was able to throw multiple cans through the kitchen window without waking me has been a real head scratcher," he said, trying to piece together how it might have happened.

"There seems to be a chemical compound on the rag. Might be chloroform or some chemical like it," Lawler surmised as he studied the cloth.

"I woke with a strangely sweet taste in my mouth and in a brain fog like you wouldn't believe." Just thinking about it brought back the taste. "I couldn't figure out why."

Now, he might have an answer.

"Does that handkerchief look familiar to you?" Liv chimed in, motioning toward the white cloth.

"It looks a lot like the one Ed keeps wiping his forehead with now that you mention it," Corbin stated. He was still keyed up from his exchange with Kellan and could use a solid workout to break up some of the tension causing his muscles to pull taut. He rolled his shoulders.

Liv walked over to the jug of water as Lawler bagged the evidence. The fact someone like Ed could have gotten the drop on Corbin sat like a lead weight in the pit of his stomach. He'd tracked some of the most dangerous poachers in the state and an older man like Ed caught him unaware? How was that even possible? Ed had to be working with someone. His mystery client? A hired hand?

"Well, this is subtle," Liv stated on a sigh. She picked something off the face of the jug. "He seems to have forgotten he shoved a business card in my face when he dropped by unannounced yesterday.

The two of them filled Lawler in on the visit.

"Did Ed say how he knew there was smoke here?" Lawler asked.

"At first, he said he heard over the radio. Then, he told you that he followed the smoke," Liv supplied.

"If you buy that excuse, I have a bridge over in Gun Barrel City for sale," Corbin quipped. He couldn't help it. He had half a mind to pay Ed a visit and shake the man down. He had to have been the one to tell Kellan about Corbin being at Liv's.

A thought struck. Was Kellan the mystery buyer? What would he want with the property?

Or maybe he just wanted rid of Liv. She still hadn't signed the divorce papers and Kellan could be trying to intimidate her into a fast exit from Lone Star Pass.

"Kellan asked for this place in the divorce," Liv informed them. "It's the reason I haven't signed the papers yet and why I need a real lawyer to look them over."

Last Corbin checked, Kellan didn't get to decide who stayed and who left the town. If anything, Corbin was even more resolved to help Liv. He hoped she wasn't too thrown off by what had happened.

And it was more than protective instincts or friendship that had him wanting to help. Could he stay and still keep his distance? Because he'd caught himself staring at her full lips more times than he cared to count this morning despite knowing just how off limits they were.

LIV HAD a stubborn streak a mile wide. She'd known it since

the third grade when one of the Baker boys had stolen her pencil and refused to give it back. She'd bided her time for weeks without retaliating. And then, when he was home with the flu, she'd raided his desk during recess. Not only did she take her pencil back—it was mechanical and had the best grip so there was no way she wasn't getting it back —but she'd taken his lucky rock too.

The Baker boy had thrown a fit when he realized his rock was missing. He'd accused her, which didn't take a rocket scientist, but the teacher had dismissed the idea saying that Liv was a model student. It was true. But the rock wasn't going back until Liv was ready to forgive the kid.

Two years later, he miraculously found it at the bottom of his backpack. She'd gotten her apology even though he was twenty-four months late and apologizing for the wrong thing. Even so, she accepted. She was stubborn not mean.

Ed had no idea what was coming to him.

"I need to talk to Ed and tell him I want to move forward with the deal," Liv announced.

"You might want to drink a cup of coffee and get the smoke smell out of your house before you make any rash decisions." Corbin's eyebrow shot up as Lawler put the new evidence in a paper bag and then inside his SUV.

"I'm not actually going through with it," she said. "I just want his folder."

"That's one way to find out who could be behind all this." Corbin caught on quickly.

"You're right about the coffee. I need caffeine almost as much as I...never mind." She almost slipped and said, *needed him.* Both were true. She couldn't imagine life without her best friend.

On a sigh, she walked over to the sheriff's SUV.

"Do you need anything else from me?" she asked. "I'd like to start airing out my house and I have a window to fix."

"The house has been cleared on my end. I'd like to walk around the property if it's all right with you," the sheriff said.

"Do whatever you need to in order to find the creep who did this," she stated. There didn't seem to be much in the way of permanent damage. Was this another warning? A way to light a fire under her backside to leave Lone Star Pass forever? Sadly, it was working. She was ready to be done with this town.

She walked over to Corbin, who was on his cell.

"I'd appreciate it if you could come out today," he said into the receiver. He was quiet for a few beats. "No, not at the ranch. I'm at a friend's place. Here, let me give you the address." Another few beats passed. "I'm at Liv Holden's place." His forehead wrinkled like he was confused. "Why not?"

She immediately knew where this was going. It was the same response she got when she tried to get grocery delivery and when she tried to get a plumber out to fix her leaky kitchen sink. Thank heaven for the internet. She'd been able to watch a few tutorials and figure it out for herself. The groceries required leaving home and interacting with people.

Since listening to this conversation would only lead to more frustration on her part, she decided to survey the damage inside. She walked to the backdoor that had been propped open. She guessed one of the firemen had done it to air the place out.

She coughed the minute she stepped inside the room. Pulling her shirt over her nose, she systematically went through the house opening windows and propping open doors. There was a slight breeze this morning, which should help speed the process along. There were a pair of fans in the hallway closet, so she pulled those out and strategically placed them to move air through the downstairs faster. Later, she could always light a candle if there was still a smell tonight. At least she had the whole day to get rid of the odor.

By the time she returned to the kitchen, she was able to lose the mouth and nose covering at least. She put on a pot of coffee and opted for a breakfast bar since her stomach was growling. She put one out for Corbin but quickly realized that wouldn't nearly be enough for him. He was almost twice her size.

Her mind snapped to the confrontation between Corbin and Kellan. Their grandfather had passed away earlier in the month, giving the land and cattle to Corbin's father while giving Kellan's dad the mineral rights. The latter was where the real money was in property ownership. In fact, most folks in Texas bought land minus the mineral rights. Having both was the equivalent of hitting the jackpot. Problem was, Corbin's dad and uncle had spent a lifetime being at odds with each other. In order for Kellan's father to drill, he had to have permission from Corbin's. The will had been set up to force them to compromise.

If people thought Liv was stubborn, they'd never met a Firebrand. There was some caveat in the will, she'd learned, that gave the land, cattle, and mineral rights to the brothers and cousins equally if they got married before their fathers could find a compromise.

Hell might truly freeze over before those men could agree on anything, let alone something worth tens of millions of dollars. The only reason Kellan's side of the family still lived on the property at all was due to a clause that said each owned their own house and the property it sat on, even if they couldn't demolish those houses to drill.

The joyous smell of coffee filled Liv's nostrils, breaking into her heavy thoughts. Based on Kellan and Corbin's earlier exchange, the family divide had grown. It was a shame, considering how close they could be. The Marshall's damage might outlive everyone, especially since the cousins were more divided than ever. They'd all been close once with the exception of a few personalities that clashed. Overall, they got along and definitely had each other's backs in a crisis. It was sad to think their grandfather had eroded all that. And for what? His own amusement? She couldn't begin to understand a man like the Marshall.

"Hey," Corbin said as he walked inside the room. "Mind if I get a cup?"

"I'm one step ahead of you, mister." She handed over the second one she'd poured along with a power bar. "It isn't much but should tide you over until I can get enough of the funk out of here to cook. I'm afraid eggs would come out tasting like smoke."

He nodded before taking a sip.

"At least the coffee isn't tainted," he said. "And it's damn good."

His gaze fixated on her bottom lip.

"You have a little right here in the corner," he said.

She slicked her tongue across her lip. Her stomach free fell when she caught the hungry look in his eyes. She'd see it once before when he'd dropped the friends routine and kissed her. Wow, she'd forced herself not to think about the kiss they'd shared after high school graduation, burying the memory down deep.

They'd been in Hank's field sitting around the campfire, nursing beers. Neither had been drinkers in high school but it seemed like the cool thing to do. She'd taken of sip of hers just to give the impression she was part of the crowd.

Later in the evening as the party started winding down and folks piled into pickup trucks, Corbin had offered to give her a ride home. She climbed in the passenger seat like she'd done dozens of times. Her phone had gone flying when she reached for the seatbelt. They'd both gone for it in the floorboard and...

The rest, as they say, was history.

The moment their lips had touched, she'd known they were in dangerous territory. The connection between them had hummed inside her as he deepened the kiss.

And then in the same moment, as though they'd had the exact same thought, they opened their eyes. Reality set in and they pulled back, but the hunger she'd seen in his eyes that night had left her wondering what might have happened. No one since Corbin had made her feel all electric impulses and sensual shivers.

Had she resigned to the fact?

The short answer...yes. Not one person since Corbin had kissed her in a way that made her bones melt and her toes curl. Not one person stirred up the kind of desire that made her feel like she'd burn up from the inside out if she didn't get more, or made her want in the same way he did. And not one person since had come close to making her fall as hard as she did that night. And now? She would most likely spend the rest of her life trying to find someone who came in a close second.

7

"Do you still think Kellan has nothing to do with what happened this morning?" Liv's question caught Corbin off guard.

"Based on his reaction to seeing me here, I have my doubts. There was a look in his eyes earlier that said he was hurting and trying to cover the fact with anger. Wish I could rule him out, though, but I can't," Corbin stated matter of fact.

"Doesn't it seem like too much of a coincidence that he showed up not long after Ed?" she asked.

"It might be my pride speaking, but I can't accept the fact Ed got the drop on me." Corbin wasn't so tired he wouldn't hear someone approaching.

"Someone might have snuck up on you and covered your face with chloroform." She involuntarily shivered at the thought.

"I'm a light sleeper. I would have heard a guy like Ed," he insisted. "Plus, how did he get up the lane without my knowledge?"

"You think the mystery client is the one?" she asked.

"I'd like to size the person up and see what they're made of." He'd been on alert last night. Granted, he'd underestimated the situation. Sleeping outside was meant to keep him away from Liv. Safe. Only a trained tracker or skilled poacher could have pulled off a sneak attack.

"Is it possible you just let your guard down and fell asleep?" She put a hand up to stop him when he started to argue. "You've been through a lot this month with losing your grandfather."

"Even so...Ed?" He must've shot a look because she smiled, and it broke up some of the tension.

"I guess you're right. He's not exactly a killer," she said. "He could bore someone to death, but that's about all."

The fact one of his cousins could be involved on Kellan's behalf crossed Corbin's mind. He didn't want to believe one of his own could pull something like this.

"For my money, I'm guessing Kellan is somehow pulling the strings," she said.

"He could be the mystery buyer for all we know, since you didn't sign the papers right away. He could be coming at you from every angle because he knows how important this place is to you," he admitted, and then he looked at her. Really looked at her. Dark circles cradled her eyes. Tension lines scored her forehead. He closed the gap between them in a couple of steps and brought his hand up to her cheek, brushing the backs of his fingers against her creamy skin. "I'm sorry you're having to go through this."

"It's not your fault," she said. "I made my bed. Now, I have to lie in it."

"You didn't ask to be treated like an outcast in the town where you grew up," he argued. "And if I know you, you tried to make the marriage work."

"I jumped into it too soon." She exhaled and it was like a

balloon deflating. "I should have known better, but I got caught up in…" She seemed to catch herself before she admitted to something she didn't want him to know.

"People make mistakes," he countered, wishing he could ease some of her pain. Heaven knew he'd made his fair share.

"Not you," she said quickly.

"I mess up pretty much every day." He was still kicking himself for a few doozies, not the least of which was how he'd handled his friendship with Liv. "Ever notice how easy it is to take something for granted?"

"Yeah, I'm afraid I have," she said, and then compressed her lips.

Or *someone,* he thought a bit more accurately. Wallowing in self-pity never fixed anything. And he didn't do regret. But if he did…it would involve Liv.

He brought his hand down onto her shoulder and then touched his forehead to hers. Being here in the kitchen with her, like this, was the most intimate moment he'd experienced in far too long. He didn't want to let himself get lost in the familiarity of his best friend, but he couldn't help how he felt. And right now, all he could think about was her full lips and how they'd feel moving against his.

Instead of sliding down that slippery slope, he cleared his throat and lifted his head up. He took another sip of coffee, figuring he could use a bathroom to splash cold water on his face and brush his teeth.

"Thanks for the coffee," he said, reverting to polite conversation. He could hear the huskiness in his own voice. Going deep with Liv would only make it that much more difficult when she disappeared from his life.

"You're welcome," she said, sounding just as affected. She brought her hand up to smooth across his chin, and then his jawline. "This probably isn't the time to bring this up but you are a beautiful person."

"You're right," he managed to say through the emotions swirling in his thoughts. "You shouldn't say stuff like that."

Pulling on all his strength, he walked out the back door to retrieve his backpack. He gave himself a mental head-shake. He needed to snap out of the attraction thing with Liv. No matter how much he couldn't stand Kellan, especially at the moment, Liv was off limits. He got caught up in pity then because he couldn't get a handyman who'd been working with the family for years to agree to come fix her window. The minute Allen had heard her name, he started backtracking.

Corbin had known she wouldn't lie to him and yet he'd somehow underestimated the situation she described. He was frustrated and embarrassed at how she was being treated. It also made him want to dig his heels in. His cell buzzed in his pocket. He pulled it out and checked the screen.

Word traveled fast in a small town. The caller was his father.

"Hello," he said, figuring he could count on one hand the number of times his father had called or texted this year. Brodie Firebrand was about as into technology as a field mouse.

"Mind if I ask where you are?" his father started right in. There was no judgment in his tone. Curiosity was a better word.

"I'm at Liv Holden's place." There was no reason to lie. "Why?"

"So, it's true," his father said, accusation laced his tone.

"I'm not sure I know what you're talking about." Corbin's defenses kicked up a few notches.

"You're with your cousin's wife." The way his father said the last word was fingernails on a chalkboard to Corbin.

"Ex," he corrected. "Their divorce is a signature away from being finalized."

The line went dead silent.

"She's being threatened and had nowhere else to turn," Corbin finally said by way of defense.

"Threatened how?" his father asked.

He gave a quick rundown of events. "You should know Kellan has been sending threatening texts. He'll be part of the investigation."

"Is that so?" The wheels were turning but Corbin had no idea what his father was thinking. The two couldn't be more different and Brodie Firebrand seemed more involved with finding ways to argue with his brother Keifer than tending to his own sons. Suffice it to say the two had never been close. The call was coming in from left field.

"It is," he said.

"What's happening to her isn't right. I don't condone it one bit," his father hedged. "But it's not our place to get involved."

"She's my friend," he said before realizing his father would never understand.

"That may be so, however—"

"You know what, Dad? I have to go. The sheriff is waving me over and I need to see what he wants," he cut in. "And since I've known Liv my entire life, I will be helping her. And other people should too. What's happening here is embarrassing and a blight on the Firebrand name."

His father didn't launch a defense. He seemed to carefully consider his next words. "As far as the window goes, I'll send someone over. I'd like for you to come home and let the law deal with the rest."

It was a good thing his father didn't issue an order because Corbin didn't want to go behind his old man's wishes.

"I'm not leaving her alone to deal with some jerk who is trying to intimidate her. What kind of person would I be if I let a bully push her around?" he defended with a little more heat than he'd intended.

"If that's how you feel, I won't ask you again. I've made my wishes clear," his father said.

"Yes, you sure have. And for the record, you should be on my side on this one." Corbin couldn't help but get in the dig.

Without saying goodbye, his father hung up. At least the man knew where Corbin stood. Conversations with the man had been few and far between. Between his father's emotional distance and the fact he'd had an affair that recently rocked the family, Corbin had no idea who the man was or what he stood for. Not now. Not before.

Corbin felt like his father was letting him down, just like he had every time his father had canceled fishing trips when they'd been kids. He couldn't remember a time growing up when he'd gone fishing with his father or grandfather for that matter. The elder Firebrands seemed too busy plotting revenge and competing against each other to spend time with their sons or grandsons. He wasn't feeling sorry for himself. It was what it was. He subscribed to a different philosophy when it came to family. If and when Corbin had children of his own, he planned to be a hands-on dad. And since life was full of irony, the only person he could see himself starting a family with was Liv.

The revelation caught him off guard, but he couldn't deny it.

Lawler was circling the perimeter as Corbin approached.

"Find anything useful out here?" he asked the lawman.

"Afraid not." He pointed toward the dry earth. "Ground is too hard for anyone to leave footprints. I'm guessing the perp came from around the house and behind your truck. Catching you off guard took some cunning, so I've pretty much counted Ed out as the offender. I'm not saying he isn't involved in some way. I just haven't made the connection yet."

"I agree about him not being the one to throw the cans inside the house." Corbin's pride couldn't take the hit. "And I agree he's somehow involved. My guess is that he's more of a puppet in this scenario."

"You have solid investigative skills and good instincts," Lawler said. "Ever think about hanging up your saddle to join law enforcement?"

"Not a day in my life," he said with a smile. Those were skills he didn't want to need.

"Kellan wouldn't be obvious enough to send those awful and mean texts if he planned on doing something like this," Corbin pointed out. "I can't put my finger on why, but he looked hurt not guilty."

Lawler nodded.

"I also just tried to get a contractor out to help with the window and as soon as he found out the work was for Liv, he backed out." Corbin would have to patch up the window himself if his dad didn't follow through with the offer to send someone. Somehow, Corbin doubted the man would keep to his word.

"Are you saying folks could be stepping in to get revenge for Kellan?" Lawler stopped looking around and focused on Corbin.

"It's possible." As much as Corbin didn't like the possibility, it was worth considering.

"Could also make it difficult to catch the perp," Lawler said matter of fact. "If folks are acting individually with no coercion, it might be harder to pick up on their trail."

"That may be so, but I'd still like to be a fly on the wall when you speak to Ed," Corbin admitted.

"Come on over to the viewing room. Can't hurt," Lawler said.

Unless, of course, Ed admitted to setting up Liv today. At that point, Corbin couldn't make any promises as to what he might do to the man. "What time?"

"I have to swing by the Perry home for a wellness check after I leave here." He glanced at his phone. "It's already coming up on noon. I have a lunch meeting with one of my deputies and then I'll head to the office and call Ed. I'll let you know when we agree on a specific time for him to come in."

"Much appreciated, Sheriff." Corbin offered a handshake, which Lawler took.

"She's been through a lot recently," Lawler stated. "She's lucky to have a friend like you to stick up for her."

Corbin nodded and offered a smile, despite feeling the exact opposite. Considering he'd pretty much been a jerk to Liv last night and he still couldn't wrap his head around her and Kellan, he didn't feel like much of a friend.

He let his ego get in the way of being a better person. All he could think about in the kitchen earlier was kissing her. He couldn't stop thinking about how her lips might feel against his, the heat, or the promise of more.

So, yeah, he was not rocking the friend zone but that needed to change.

Liv stood in her kitchen, staring at the broken window. Part of her wanted to declare war. The other, more sensible, part wanted to move on and never look back at Lone Star Pass. It was time, right? To put down roots somewhere else. The thought of leaving the house she'd shared with her mother nearly gutted Liv.

Then there was the part about leaving Corbin that felt like she was ripping out an appendage. She needed to be done here. She sighed. Sticking around that man would only lead to trouble. The kiss they'd almost shared, but didn't had put her on notice. Wanting more from Corbin was the worst of bad ideas. They couldn't even remain friends under the circumstances. Talk about an impossible situation.

She loved Texas and she loved this town. At least, she had before it had turned on her and made her feel unwelcome. But did she love the man?

Liv gave herself a mental headshake. It was far too early in the day for deep questions. She drained the contents of her coffee cup, thinking a meal would be nice. The breakfast bar had held her this long, but it was waning and she needed sustenance.

She opened the fridge door. There wasn't much in there to work with. Certainly not enough to cook a decent meal. Could they call in an order and pick it up in town? Her heart clenched at the thought of running into anyone, especially while she was with Corbin. Okay, so that was a bad idea.

The sound of vehicles coming up the drive got her feet moving to the living room and her heart pounding. What now?

Two trucks she recognized as belonging to Corbin's

family ranch drove toward her, and then parked side-by-side.

Corbin's mother exited the passenger side of one of the trucks that his oldest brother Adam had been driving. Brax parked alongside his brother as Corbin made a beeline toward them. The man should be on his honeymoon except his new bride had to resume her tour. She figured he needed backup, so she barreled out the front door as Sheriff Lawler waved and pulled away.

Lucia Firebrand was short and round, and one of the kindest people Liv had ever met on the occasions she'd been to the ranch. Her Italian heritage explained how so many of her sons inherited dark eyes and hair.

The older woman was scurrying toward the house, her arms full with a box and something stacked inside. The smile on her face allowed Liv to exhale.

"We came as soon as we heard," Mrs. Firebrand said, practically beaming.

"I'm confused." Liv stopped in her tracks. From all appearances the cavalry had arrived. But why would they help her?

She could've sworn her mouth hit the ground as she watched Adam and Brax embrace their brother before unloading supplies from the back of a truck.

"How about we take this into the kitchen?" Mrs. Firebrand winked as she scurried past.

Liv had to shake it off for a hot second. She turned tail and hurried to the front door so she could open it. Mrs. Firebrand thanked her as she walked right on past like helping out was an everyday occurrence. Honestly, it probably was for her.

The guys outside were even more shocking. It was common knowledge that Firebrands stuck together. Mess with one and they came running. Of course, with the Marshall gone and conflict arising from his will, the family could be more divided than ever.

"Please, make yourself at home," Liv said to Mrs. Firebrand. "I have one question to ask Corbin and I'll be right back."

"Take your time." The sound of the fridge door opening and closing along with Mrs. Firebrand's humming warmed Liv's heart. This place had been empty and quiet far too long. It was like someone was finally breathing life back into the home—a home she loved.

Liv made a beeline for Corbin, who was standing with his brothers talking like this morning hadn't just been the worst on record. It might not actually have been worse but was definitely top ten on her list.

The sun was shining, heating the crown of her head as she approached. She must've looked confused as all get out because all three men smiled.

At six-feet-one-inches, Brax was the shortest in the family. He had a solid build, just like the others, and eyes so blue they popped. His dirty brown hair was the lightest of the others and now the family knew why. He was the product of an affair their father had had years ago. Mrs. Firebrand had been able to look past it and take him in, raising him as her own and loving him just the same. Then, there was Adam. His hair was so dark it was almost black. He had piercing pale blue eyes with just enough scruff on his chin for women to consider him sexy. He was six-feet-three-inches of solid muscle. Built much like the others. Chiseled jawlines and improbable bodies were pretty much a hallmark of the Firebrand men.

And yet, Corbin had always stood out as the best looking out of all of them on both sides of the family, in her opinion.

He was the quiet thinker of the group and there was something incredibly sexy about it. He took his time when he followed through on anything, and it made her wonder how slow he would take other things...bedroom things. Her stomach flip-flopped just thinking about it.

Since that line of thinking was as productive as shutting off her neighbor's water when her own house flooded, she gave herself a mental shake and did her level best to move on.

8

"Good to see you again, Liv," Adam said first and Brax agreed.

Corbin's chest nearly burst with pride for his family showing up for him like this, especially after his conversation with his father. Liv seemed especially shocked and he understood the reason. Kellan's side of the family had been anything but cordial, whereas Corbin's seemed ready to welcome her with open arms.

"I-uh-um," she stammered, "agree. So good to see you both."

She ducked, and he realized she was trying to hide the fact she was tearing up. His chest squeezed and it dawned on him how lonely she must have felt in the past couple of years. Losing her mother and then their friendship looked to have taken a toll.

"Mom brought enough food to feed an army and my brothers are here to fix the window," Corbin said with a smile.

"I'm grateful," she said quickly. "Just..."

She seemed to be searching for the right word.

"Shocked?" he said on her behalf. Adam and Brax chuckled.

"If I'm honest? Yes. Very." At least she'd found her voice now and she raised her chin. Tears welled in her eyes but she held them at bay.

"We're not like the other side of the family," Adam stated. "We don't turn our backs on people we care about."

"Thank you." The gratitude in her voice and her eyes melted a little more of the ice encasing Corbin's heart.

It felt good to do the right thing. Helping Liv most definitely fell into that category.

"If you're ready, we'll get to work," Brax said with a smile.

The fact his brothers had come ready to pitch in meant more than Corbin could express. "I'll show you to the kitchen."

Corbin grabbed a toolbox and walked around the back of the house.

"Seriously, what made you decide to come help out?" Liv asked Adam. "I know you and Kellan don't get along, but I also realize you wouldn't do this out of spite."

"It's messed up what happened here this morning," Adam admitted. "But what gets me is that no one in town is willing to help you. Firebrands aren't any better than anyone else and don't deserve special treatment."

The anger in his brother's voice at the injustice was one of many reasons Corbin respected the hell out of his family.

"Thanks," Liv said, tucking her chin to her chest. For a split-second, Corbin thought she might be trying to cover for tears again. He wouldn't blame her for crying after all she'd been through. Plus, she had to be tired. "I have an interview tomorrow morning in Dallas. Soon enough I'll be out of everyone's hair."

"Shame," Adam said. "I know you and Corbin go way back. I'm sure he'll miss you."

No response came. She looked like she didn't know how to respond.

"He'll be better off when I'm gone," she said so low Corbin almost didn't hear it before excusing herself and disappearing into the house.

"I do realize you were just being polite, but thank you," Corbin said to Adam.

He shook his head. "She's important to you, Corbin. You would never risk driving another wedge in between members of the family if she wasn't."

"No wedge necessary," Corbin defended. "I'm just helping someone who needs it on her way to another life."

Dallas was far and his life was in Lone Star Pass. He worked six days a week, seven during calving season. Their strained friendship would die on the vine with the distance she was about to put between them under the best of circumstances. For the time she remained, he resolved to set his ego aside and be there for her. She had always been a small-town girl, so the move to a big city must be scary. She couldn't have picked a more different life, opposite extremes. The only common thread was both places were still in Texas.

A text came in while his brothers went to work. Corbin checked the screen.

Two o'clock?

Corbin responded to the sheriff's text with a *Yes*.

See you in my office.

Ed had sure better come ready to reveal who he was representing or risk spending time behind bars himself. Lawler didn't seem amused and he wouldn't put up with any bull. The timing of the intimidation tactics was suspect, considering someone seemed desperate to get hold of this property. Kellan making a play for it was purely meant to hurt Liv. He would most likely bulldoze the place just to destroy any good memories she had of Lone Star Pass.

Corbin sent a 'thumbs up' via text and then pocketed his cell phone. He looked up to find his brothers staring at him.

"Who was that?" Brax asked.

"Lawler is bringing Ed Roberts in for questioning. Said we could come listen in," Corbin stated before filling them in on the Realtor's tie to the place.

Brax cocked an eyebrow. "Let's hope this whole ordeal isn't somehow tied back to our cousin."

Adam gave a look of agreement.

"Kellan sent some incriminating texts," Corbin supplied.

"Like threats?" Adam asked.

"Not 'like' threats. They were pointed threats," Corbin stated.

"I'm surprised he would pull something like that, but I guess I should have known." Adam shook his head as he worked. "He leads with his temper and I knew it would come back to bite him someday."

"The day of reckoning might be now," Brax agreed.

"Let's hope they were idle," Corbin stated. "Or he might just end up in jail."

"And he would deserve it if he was responsible for any of this," Adam agreed.

Corbin filled his brother in on the raccoon.

"Liv should sign out a restraining order against him, if that's the case," Adam stated. "I'd like to think Kellan is honorable and sent those texts just to blow off steam out of anger, but if he acted on it..."

Adam's voice seethed.

"Let's see where the trail with Ed leads before we get too

worked up," Corbin said. He needed all the facts before he made a judgment. Keeping a level head had kept him from making huge errors in judgment in his life. Anger caused people to react. It made logical thinking nearly impossible. "He was here, you know. We had a dust up."

"Kellan?" Adam sounded as shocked as Corbin had been.

He nodded. "Showed up full of fire. Threatened me. Told me that he'd take it up with me back at the ranch before he split. Needless to say, I told him to bring it on."

Corbin might not be hot-tempered, and he liked to have all the facts before making a decision, but he didn't back down from anyone. And that went double for his any one of his cousins.

"This is about the will," Adam stated, and it was easy to see his blood pressure was rising. "Our dads didn't need a reason to fight before all this started. They've been at each other's throats since before I was born. Now, that the Marshall has given them one, there'll be no peace until this is settled."

"It is settled as far as I'm concerned," Corbin said. "The will is a legal document and they are at a standstill. There isn't much else to be said. Of course, the Marshall should have done the right thing in the first place and split everything down the middle but he didn't. This is what we're stuck with and unless Uncle Keif can come to the table with a solid offer as to why we should allow him to drill on our land, he's out of luck."

"They would ruin the cattle business if grandfather had given it to them. He knew it and that's why he split up the inheritance the way he did," Adam said. "I'm not saying I agree one way or the other, but I do understand his reasoning."

"You won't get any argument out of me there," Brax chimed in as he measured the window. "But I still think we should have gotten half the mineral rights."

"Well, there's a way to make that happen," Adam stated, spreading out the glass cutting supplies consisting of a cutting wheel, pliers, and nippers.

"You're talking about all of us being married before Dad and Uncle Keifer agree on a solution," Corbin stated, thinking how perfect a match Adam and Prudence were as the two of them had recently found real love. Then there was his brother Brax. He'd found the love of his life in Raleigh, a hometown girl done good in the country music business. "No, thanks. And, besides, that's not going to happen. Us single men are the majority by far."

"Our dad and uncle will agree on anything when hell freezes over," Brax stated, cutting the glass.

Hanging out with his brothers was nice. On the ranch, they all had their respective jobs, which meant a whole lot of alone time. Normally, Corbin preferred it that way. Now, he was appreciating the company.

"We can take shifts tonight," Brax said, changing the subject as he managed the perfect cut of glass. "If you want us to come hang out here. It's not like I can be with Raleigh yet while she's back on tour."

"Never hurts to have a second set of eyes," Adam agreed.

"I appreciate the thought, but I won't be caught off guard again." He went over the details of the chloroform and how he'd been surprised. "The person caught me unaware and that's the only reason he got the best of me. Won't happen twice."

He'd never been more certain of anything in his life.

"If Liv was planning to stick around, I'd tell her to get an alarm system and a dog," Brax stated. "And I have no doubt no one will get past you tonight."

"It'll be early to bed and early to rise for Liv." Rancher hours, Corbin thought. He didn't mind. In fact, he preferred them. But no sleep for him. He had no plans to let his guard down. "And you're right about all three."

Dogs were the best at raising the signal if anyone was on the property. There were several dogs around the ranch, each had run of the mill. The barn had A/C and the dogs could sleep inside if they wanted.

Corbin should suggest getting a dog to Liv when she moved into the city. Again, the thought of her leaving gutted him. He was allowing himself to get too attached. *Not cool, Firebrand.* Keeping her in the friend zone was proving more difficult than he expected.

HAVING Mrs. Firebrand and the others here was the first time this place had felt like home in too long, Liv thought as she changed clothes and washed her face. The day was only starting in some respects and yet it felt like she'd been awake for two days already.

She checked the bags under her eyes, covering them up with a little highlighter. Lip gloss rounded out her look after she pinched her cheeks, trying to bring some life back in her face. Hot mess was a kind description when she caught sight of herself in the mirror.

Liv ran a brush through her hair before pulling it off her face in a low ponytail. Her outfit of blue jeans and a halter top was a huge improvement over her t-shirt and pajama bottoms, and she was beginning to feel human again.

Then there was the fact she had people in her corner

now. Relief wasn't nearly big enough a word to cover how she felt and it was then that she realized how lonely she'd been. She could hear the guys working downstairs and don't even get her started on the smells wafting upstairs from the kitchen. Mrs. Firebrand was the most amazing cook.

Her thoughts drifted to recent events and she realized how vulnerable she'd been. If someone wanted her dead, they'd proven last night they could get to her. Not anymore, she thought. There was no way Corbin would allow that to happen on his watch twice.

Were these pranks? Threats? Was someone trying to make her uncomfortable? Scared?

"Food's ready," Mrs. Firebrand's singsong voice traveled through the house. That woman was everything home and hearth.

Liv gave herself a final mirror check before heading down. Her stomach had been reminding her it was lunchtime for a solid twenty minutes. Good food didn't need to be rushed, though. And Mrs. Firebrand's cooking was the best.

"I hope you like manicotti and garlic bread," Mrs. Firebrand said as she stood in front of the oven.

"Is that a joke? Homemade anything sounds amazing and this kitchen smells like heaven despite what happened this morning," Liv said. She took in a deep breath.

The older woman beamed with pride. Corbin's mother was in stark contrast to Liv's former mother-in-law on Kellan's side of the family. Jackie Firebrand had fake nails and wore extensions. She carried one of those purse dogs around like it was a baby. And she fussed over it endlessly. The image of her as a rancher's wife didn't jibe. Jackie was from Houston and came from oil money. She knew the ropes and had considered Keifer Firebrand 'a catch.'

Lucia Firebrand, on the other hand, was warm and kind and motherly. The only thing she and her sister-in-law had in common was the last name Firebrand.

"I'm happy to hear because I packed your freezer and fridge with plenty more," she said.

"I can't thank you enough, Mrs. Firebrand." The older woman was putting herself in a sticky situation with her in-laws in coming here and possibly her own husband as well.

"Please, call me Lucia," she said, those deep brown eyes so warm and welcoming. Despite a few wrinkles, she was a beautiful woman, inside and out. And wasn't that where true beauty began anyway? On the inside?

Corbin was a beautiful man. Although, he would never think of himself in this light. Despite family meaning everything to him, he was helping her. He was the kind of person who could be counted on no matter the circumstances. He was a decent human being and shared the same sense of humor as her. But it was his mind she'd been most drawn to. He was intelligent beyond most. He didn't have a truly wicked bone in his body and his even temper proved one of his best assets. Forget the man was so hot he could melt butter on any part of his body...okay, time to reign her thoughts in. Thinking about hot butter anywhere on Corbin's body crossed a line she didn't need to be anywhere near.

"Tell me about this job interview you have," Lucia began as she plated food.

Liv cleared her throat trying to ease some of the sudden dryness. Better yet, she grabbed a bottle of water from the fridge and took a couple of sips.

"It'll be using my degree," Liv started.

"Sounds promising," Lucia said.

"I'll get to work with kids one-on-one who have learning

difficulties in a clinical setting," she continued. "My specialty is working with dyslexic children and helping them develop strategies to cope so they can remain in class with their peers."

"That's important work." Lucia nodded her approval and smiled. When she spoke, her hands moved as quickly as her tongue, and Liv found herself smiling at the older woman's enthusiasm.

Liv had missed being around Corbin's mother. Once she got serious with Kellan, Liv had stuck to the 'other' side of the cattle ranch. Marshall Firebrand had built two equally impressive barns and two beautiful homes on the property for his sons. It was as though a line had been drawn down the middle of the property and each house stayed on their side.

Looking back on it now, it was strange but growing up with it she never thought twice. Funny how getting used to something made it seem normal. Their family situation was anything but.

For a split second, Liv felt the urge to apologize to Lucia for crossing the line to the other side. She shelved the idea when the older woman called the guys in to wash up for lunch. The three came through the back door faster than a mouse could say the word, *cheese.*

"This smell is a huge improvement over this morning," Corbin said, stepping aside to allow his brothers to grab a plate first.

There were four seats at her table in the eat-in kitchen. She grabbed a folding chair from her hall closet and joined the others.

"No reason to go out of your way," Lucia said, waving her hands in the air. "I already ate before I came."

"I don't mind," Liv stated. "Come join us."

Lucia threw a kitchen towel over her shoulder and took a seat. "Did you know the Paisleys have been trying to start a good quality program for children with learning challenges right here in Lone Star Pass?"

"No, I didn't." Liv smiled, thinking there was no way she was sticking around after everything that had happened. Plus, no one would hire her. All Kellan or his family had to do was flex a little bit and even the Paisleys would cower.

"If they had a person who was trained to work with the children, they'd probably be able to realize their dream." Lucia winked. "I'm about to help them with a fundraiser next month and I could give them a call if you'd like."

Corbin seemed to catch on to the implication.

"Liv already has a job lined up," he said.

"She hasn't even interviewed yet," his mother said like she was quietly shushing a kid for speaking out of turn.

Corbin shot his mother a confused look.

Lucia smiled in return and fired off another wink. Corbin excused himself from the table and walked out the back door.

Liv had half a mind to follow him and tell him that she had no plans to stick around and ruin his life any more than she already had, but Adam beat her to the punch. She didn't want to intrude on their private conversation, so she stayed put, wishing she had the nerve to go tell him.

9

"I love Mom with all my heart, but her knack for interfering in our lives needs to stop," Corbin said to his brother. "No disrespect intended."

Adam put his hands in the air, palms up, in the surrender position.

"You are correct," he said. "She won't, though."

"Trying to convince Liv to stay here when the town has turned on her isn't going to help her situation," Corbin continued. His hands fisted at his sides thinking about it and he started pacing the length of the house.

"People will get over it in time," Adam protested.

"Whoa, there. Whose side are you on?" Corbin asked.

"I'm not picking between my mother and my brother if that's what you're asking." Adam made a show of acting innocent. He was trying to lighten the mood and Corbin appreciated the gesture even if it did fall flat.

"I know Mom is trying to be helpful," Corbin relented.

"It's why she rounded us up and asked if we would accompany her over here in the first place," Adam stated.

"This was her idea?" Corbin didn't hide his shock. "Dad called."

"We know about that too," Adam said.

"He was a jerk." Corbin probably didn't have to tell his brother that part.

"I figured," Adam said.

"Wait. How did you know he called?" Corbin asked, figuring he might know the answer.

"Mom overheard the conversation," Adam admitted. "The way I see it, if Dad and Uncle Keif hadn't been just as they are, then none of us would be as close—we wouldn't have had to band together to look out for each other. Heaven knows we've all taken second place to their lifelong feud."

"We aren't any better with Kellan and some of our cousins," Corbin pointed out.

Adam compressed his lips into a frown.

"I take responsibility there. Kellan knows how to push my buttons. Always has and probably always will," Adam admitted.

"He's a jerk," Corbin agreed.

"When it comes to him, I'm probably not much better." Adam's admission surprised Corbin.

"I'd say you're a whole lot better on every level in comparison to Kellan. He's having someone pushed out of town for kicks," Corbin said.

"He's in the wrong. There's no two ways about it," Adam said. "And he shouldn't get away with throwing his weight around if that's what is happening."

"The town shouldn't cater to any one of us. We're a bunch of cattle ranchers, not movie stars or celebrities." Corbin walked back his statement when he said, "Except for

Raleigh. She's a full-blown country sensation now with her new single, *The Loft*."

Adam nodded and he practically beamed with pride. The 'loft' Raleigh wrote the song about happened to be on their side of the family's property. Apparently, her and Brax's romance sparked there but she'd spent countless hours in the barn's loft as a kid developing her songwriting skills. Now, Raleigh was a local girl who'd done good, and her and Brax were planning their honeymoon as soon as she got a break from touring.

"Speaking of Raleigh, when does Brax leave for the tour?" Corbin asked, figuring a change in subject might stop him from wearing a path in Liv's backyard.

"Wednesday, I think. Don't quote me on that," Adam said. He put his hand on Corbin's shoulder. "I know how much you can overthink a situation. Liv is a grown woman who is capable of taking care of herself. She wouldn't jump on a suggestion of Mom's lightly or for the wrong reasons."

Corbin shot his brother a look.

"She might have made a mistake in marrying Kellan," he defended. "But I'm guessing there's more to it than meets the eye." Adam threw his hands in the air. "Just my opinion, though."

"It was a doozie of a misstep," Corbin agreed.

"Don't we all screw up at times? I sure as hell know that I'm not perfect. Some come from actions and then others come from not taking a risk in the first place." Adam's words sank like a lead weight in Corbin's stomach. His brother's point was taken and received. He was saying at least Liv tried.

Could Corbin say the same thing?

He'd been close to marrying Dani. He'd asked. She'd accepted. And then he'd done an about face the minute he realized he was going down the wrong path. Gut instinct had kicked in and he just knew if he followed through with the wedding plans that he'd be miserable for the rest of his life. Her deception made walking away easy, but they'd been together for years and he'd gotten comfortable. Had he ever really loved her, though?

"I like my freedom," Corbin defended, despite Adam not accusing him of anything.

"Wasn't talking about you." Adam smirked.

Corbin pinched the bridge of his nose trying to stem the headache forming. He stopped pacing long enough to meet his brother's gaze. "I appreciate all of you, especially Mom, for what she's doing to make Liv feel welcome again. I don't think she's felt that in a long time."

"Too bad. She's a good person. But you need to relax. Let's go inside and finish up lunch," Adam said.

"Easy for you to say. You're not responsible for someone's life." Corbin realized what he'd just said a little too late to stop the train from leaving the tracks. He put his hands up. "Can we forget I said that? Chalk it up to me making another mistake?"

Adam laughed but there was a weariness to his eyes that hadn't been there before. He'd been through quite an ordeal in finding out he was a father, and that his baby was a target. His ex had never told him about the pregnancy. She was murdered shortly after the birth and his now wife ended up helping him save the little girl. So, there it was. Adam was probably still trying to recover from the shock of what had happened almost a month later. He'd been stabbed in the process of saving his child and, thanks to be healthy as a horse in the wild, he was recovering. Plus, he was taking care of a newborn, which could also account for the dark circles under his eyes.

"Remember what I said about being too inside your own head, okay?" Adam opened the door.

"I'll do my best." Corbin stepped into the kitchen and the scene was a gut punch. His mother, his brother, and his best friend all at the table in easy conversation, looking like they were enjoying each other's company.

Granted, his mother was social and could probably entertain a tree. She glanced up and smiled at him so warmly it was hard to be mad at her for interfering. Plus, she was going out of her way to make Liv feel welcome in a town that had turned their backs on her. He couldn't be mad at his mother.

"Should I head back to the ranch to give Prudence a break with my grandchild?" Becoming a grandmother looked good on her and she relished the role. The fact she finally had a little girl to spoil added to her enjoyment. She'd made the joke several times during their childhood that she kept having children in order to bring home a pink bundle one day.

"Give us five minutes to finish setting the window and we can all go," Adam said.

Corbin checked his phone.

"We should probably head out at the same time if we want to hear Lawler interview Ed," Corbin said to Liv.

The smile faded from her lips—lips he wanted to feel moving against his own like he'd imagined a dozen times already. He shoved the thought down deep. It had no place in their friendship, and he had every intention of being a better friend to her than this.

"THANK you doesn't begin to cover everything you did and

are doing for me today," Liv said as she walked the trio out alongside Corbin.

The window was fixed. The house, the downstairs at least, smelled like homemade pasta, sauce, and garlic bread instead of smoke. The place felt totally different with the family together. It finally felt like a home instead of a house with history.

"I'd like to swing by later to check on you, if it's okay," Lucia said as she turned around in front of the truck she'd been driven there in.

"Are you sure?" Liv didn't mean to question Lucia's intentions. They were pure as Colorado snow in December. She just hadn't figured that anyone would want to be associated with her for too long.

"Positive." Lucia threw her hands up. "You practically grew up at the ranch and that makes you my family. Famiglia takes care of each other."

Lucia brought Liv into the warmest embrace. So much so, that Liv ducked her head, chin to chest, so no one would see the moisture gathering in her eyes. She was tougher than this and yet Lucia seemed to know how to shred all Liv's defenses, leaving her a virtual puddle of emotion. Or had it just been *that* long since Liv had had a mother in her life?

The latter was probably true. It had been a long time since Liv had been brought into a motherly hug or made to feel like she was part of a family. Jackie had never taken to Liv. Her mother-in-law had snubbed her nose at Liv from the moment she'd walked into the woman's living room.

But then, few people were probably good enough for one of her sons, least of all a woman with no position or standing in the community. All Liv had was herself to offer and, looking back, she realized she didn't give much of that to Kellan either. Maybe Jackie was right not to get too close to Liv. Besides, the two had very little in common and never would.

"Think about what I said about the Paisleys," Lucia reminded with another wink. "You could really help them get their program off the ground. As it is now, folks have to drive all the way into Austin for help and, as you know, that's not always feasible. You could help a lot of kids in the area if you stayed."

No pressure, Liv thought with a laugh.

"I'll consider it," she said mostly to appease Lucia. Her heart wasn't into staying anywhere she wasn't wanted, and the town had been clear where they stood.

"Sometimes, the best way to put out a fire is with fire." Lucia gestured with her hands before turning toward the truck. She was in the passenger seat and ready to go before Liv could mount a coherent response.

And then it dawned on her. A Firebrand, namely Lucia, could stand up to another Firebrand, Kellan and his family. She understood the meaning now. All she could do at this point was smile and wave.

"I'll just lock up and then we can get on the road," she said to Corbin as a piece of her heart shredded watching his family pull away. His mother would be back later and quite possibly a few of the others.

"I can help close up the windows," he said, following her inside.

Liv grabbed her cell, keys, and purse. She closed windows on the ground floor while he jogged upstairs. She could keep the fans running and that should help air the place out. A shiver raced down her back at thinking what a close call they'd had this morning. Corbin had been blindsided and that wasn't an easy feat. The perp could so easily have lit the house on fire and smoke inhalation could have killed Liv in her sleep. She made a mental note to check the batteries in the smoke alarms. Had she let them run out. Didn't they beep when that happened?

Of course, she'd been preoccupied when she'd come back here. And, yes, her thoughts had drifted to Corbin more than she wanted to admit. All of which fell under the category of *Water Under the Bridge* now.

"All the windows are closed upstairs," Corbin said as he walked down. The boards creaked and groaned underneath his weight. "And, don't worry, I'm planning on staying awake tonight. I'll grab a nap when we get back from Lawler's office so I'll be ready to go."

"I'd stay up with you, but—"

"You have an important interview in the morning. Plus, I'm telling you that I'll be awake so you can sleep. After recent events, I figured you'd be on full alert," he said.

"I was just thinking how easy it would have been for this morning to have turned out differently," she said as she met him at the front door.

He followed her out and she locked it.

Corbin issued a sigh. "I've gone over and over it in my mind trying to figure out why I let it happen."

"It's not your fault," she countered.

"I was being stubborn," he said. "I should have been inside the house and then I would have heard the window breaking. No one would have been able to get to me either. Sleeping outside with my truck windows open left me vulnerable. I didn't realize what I was dealing with before. Now, I'm prepared."

She walked to his truck and he opened the passenger door for her. When she looked into his eyes, all she could see was torment.

"You don't know how things might have turned out if you hadn't been here at all," she said, bringing her hand up to touch his face. Touching him came so naturally and felt so right. Convincing her heart she needed to keep a distance was next to impossible when he was this close.

She pushed up onto her tiptoes and pressed her lips against cheek. The contact might have only happened for a few seconds, but her body hummed with electricity long after. She didn't dare look into his eyes when she was feeling this vulnerable. She couldn't risk it, couldn't risk the damage to her heart.

But when his hand came up to her chin to lift her face toward his, she had no choice.

"Corbin," she said. Her protest barely a whisper.

"I want you to look at me," he said, and his voice was gravelly and deep.

Heaven help her because she was in trouble. The minute she glanced up, he held her gaze. There was so much pull in that one look, she couldn't force herself to look away.

"What?" she finally managed to say. Her throat had dried up, making the simple act of speaking feel like she was dredging through quicksand.

His eyes glittered with something that looked a whole lot like need, causing her breath to quicken and her pulse to climb.

Walking away right now while there was a shred of hope she was still able would be the smartest play. Could she, though?

"We can't do this," he said so low she barely heard him.

She took a step back but he captured her wrist in his hand.

"Hold on," he said, his voice gravelly.

10

"You're beautiful." Corbin released her wrist before bringing his hand up to brush a few loose tendrils of hair off Liv's face.

He'd noticed her habit of looking away anytime someone complimented her. When they were kids, she would kick the dirt to draw attention away; in high school, she started the habit of ducking her head; and now, she averted her eyes. Small movements that gave her discomfort with attention away.

She was honest to a fault, a quality more people should embrace. And those were just a few of her attributes that he admired.

"Don't say stuff like that to me, Corbin." Again, she dropped her gaze.

"Why not? I've been thinking it for so long I can't even remember when it started. Maybe I should have said what was on my mind years ago and—"

His cell buzzed, breaking into the moment happening between them. It was probably for the best because in the heat of the moment he'd almost confessed something she didn't need to hear. Nothing could be done about his feelings now. He should have acted on them in the past. Because those had him falling in love with her in high school. Corbin might overthink a problem, but he'd never been one for regret. The decision to put their friendship above a relationship would haunt him for the rest of his life.

He fished his cell out of his back pocket and glanced at the screen.

Liv gasped when she saw Lawler's name.

"Hello," Corbin said and then explained the call was on speaker. "Liv is standing right here."

"I thought you'd be on your way to my office by now." Lawler sounded surprised.

"We're standing in front of my truck, about to get inside," Corbin said. He could hear the huskiness in his own voice and tried to cover with a cough.

"Don't bother," Lawler said, an ominous quality hung in the air. "Ed's body was found floating in Lake Red."

"He drowned?" Corbin tried to wrap his mind around this development.

"Shot in the chest at point blank range," Lawler supplied and his voice was laced with compassion.

"Ed was murdered?" Liv said quietly.

"I'm afraid so," Lawler said. "News is already spreading like wildfire thanks to the Harris family. They found him while taking their grandkids fishing and everyone was pretty traumatized."

"A story like this one would travel fast in a small town." Liv glanced around like someone might be waiting in the trees to get to her.

It couldn't be ruled out. But if someone wanted her dead, wouldn't they have done it this morning? Why wait?

Standing so close, it was a little too easy to loop his arm

around her waist and pull her toward him. She leaned into his body and he could feel hers trembling as he urged them toward the house, toward shelter.

"There's no reason for either of you to come to my office now but know that I'm going to increase patrol around your home," Lawler said as Corbin's phone started blowing up with texts. Proof positive that news had already traveled fast.

"Thank you for letting us know," Corbin said as they reached the front door. He needed to get Liv inside and then come up with a plan. Ed might have been a jerk but there was no way he deserved to have his life cut short.

"I don't normally comment on an ongoing investigation, but this is an exception. Given this development, it might be a good idea to keep a low profile for a few days. Stay in as much as possible. Stick together," Lawler said.

"Will do," Corbin said.

The fact Liv had clamped her mouth shut wasn't a good sign. Naturally, she would be scared but her skin had paled. Was she in shock?

Corbin ended the call with the sheriff as she fumbled for her house key. When she brought it out of her purse, her hand shook.

"I can do that," Corbin said.

"Thank you." She placed the key in his palm.

He unlocked the door, and took a look around before following her inside. She dropped her purse two steps in. And then she spun around to face him. The wild look in her eyes said she was about to do something she might regret later. Caught in the same force field, all he could do was surrender to it, to her.

He closed the distance between them in two strides and she threw her arms around his neck with the urgency of a sailboat tossing and anchor in a windstorm. Her eyes said there was a storm brewing, and a dangerous one at that.

This would be a good time to take a step back and think over the consequences, except that Corbin couldn't... *wouldn't* do that. Instead, he brought his hands up to cup Liv's cheeks. His lips moved toward hers, stopping halfway there.

She responded to his lightest touch. He searched for hesitation in her eyes. Her lips would taste like the dark roast coffee they'd had after lunch. Fog filled his mind, trying to push out rational thought—thought that reminded him she was off limits.

There would be so much heat and passion if they kissed. Corbin's imagination went wild as to what sex might be like with Liv. He probably should rein in his thoughts, except that would be impossible as she leaned into him, her body flush with his.

Every breath, every movement served to increase the tension cording his muscles like a spring. She dropped her hands to his shoulders where her fingernails dug in like she was trying to ground herself.

The electricity humming through his body kicked up a few notches as their lips inched closer. All his warning flares lit up at the same time, warning him to stop before they both hit the point of no return.

The pull was too strong. The moment happening to them had taken on a life of its own and he had no power to stop it.

LIV HAD the fleeting thought she should find a way to take a step back before they couldn't go back. Willpower wasn't normally something she had a difficult time with…until now. Until Corbin. A kiss had been more than a decade in the making and she had no doubt it would be so hot that her bones would melt. There was nothing to do but surrender to the tide coursing over her and through her, threatening to consume her in bliss while drowning out all the horrible things happening around her. But their lips never touched.

"Liv." Corbin said her name, his lips moving so close to hers that she could practically feel them. Her name rolling off his tongue was about the sweetest sound she'd ever heard.

The thought he might put the brakes on this thing happening between them caused her to loop her arms around his neck and clasp her fingers together. Electricity charged the air as her body ached for more in every possible place it could.

"Liv," he repeated, breathless this time. He managed to pull back enough to rest his forehead on hers as they both panted for air.

They hadn't even kissed and she could scarcely catch her breath. She could only imagine how mind-blowing sex would be. She didn't dare go there, not even hypothetically.

"I know," she finally said when she could catch her breath enough to manage words. "We don't need to say it."

"How do you know that's what I was going to say?" He cracked a smile but didn't budge.

"Wasn't it?" she asked, thinking he'd always liked to tease her by throwing a fastball when she expected a curve.

"No. As a matter of fact, it wasn't. But you'll never know now because I plan to take it to my grave," he teased. He had a way of lightening the most intense mood, but she could see the strain in his eyes.

"Remember that time I came to school wearing my shirt inside-out?" she asked.

"Wasn't that in, like, fourth grade?" he asked.

"Yes. And a group of kids made fun of me. Relentlessly as I remember," she noted.

"They were jerks," he said.

"True," she admitted. "I thought you were going to slam Hank Jr against the wall when he did that awful impression of me." She paused at the memory. "But, what did you do instead?"

"Not much," he said. "I'm sure it was nothing."

"No, you don't. I'm not letting you get away with being too humble to admit you were my knight in shining armor," she warned. "You didn't have to fight anyone. All you did was turn your shirt inside out, and then half the kids showed up to school the next day doing the same."

He shrugged. "Anyone would've done it. The kids needed to be shown how cool it was."

"They looked up to you, your brothers, and your cousins," she said. The reverse was happening to her now, but this wasn't the time to bring it up again. In fact, she didn't want to think about it either.

"Adam saw what we'd done, and he was the first to follow," Corbin said.

"Your brother has always had your back," she said. "I always wondered if you guys were so close because you had to band together against your father." She flashed eyes at him. "No offense to him."

"He's a decent rancher but the man was a terrible father," Corbin said. Mom more than made up for it," he quickly added. "And, look, it's not like we had it hard. We had food on the table and a loving mother. We were close-knit and my brothers always had my back. I have no complaints."

She'd never been able to imagine what that was like until that day in fourth grade when Corbin had had hers.

Liv prided herself on being able to take care of herself and never needing anyone to survive. And yet, everyone needed at least one person in their corner.

"You were special back then and you are now, Corbin." She tapped on his chest with her index finger. It went without saying his body was all muscle. Tapping him was like poking a brick. Again, her mind snapped to a place she probably shouldn't allow. One that had her wondering how amazing his body would feel against hers.

She performed a mental headshake, trying to loosen the image stamped in her thoughts, trying to take root there. The one where they were lying in bed, tangled in the sheets. It was late morning on a lazy Sunday and they'd just had breakfast in bed, enough fuel for round two, or three. She'd lost count.

Corbin was studying her, she realized, with a smirk on his face.

"What are you thinking right now?" he asked.

"Nothing. No one," she stammered. "What did you say?"

"I didn't. You were telling me what an awful kid I used to be," he teased and his eyes lit up—eyes that were a lifeline in a raging storm.

"Life sure seemed a lot easier back then," she admitted, except that wasn't completely true.

He came so close to bringing his mouth down hard on hers that her body hummed with need. She had no doubt the act of kissing Corbin would ruin her for other men for the rest of her life.

When he took in a deep breath this time, he said, "I

don't know. I can think of a few things about being an adult I wouldn't want to give up."

Her cheeks flamed. Trying to cover wouldn't do any good. She'd been thinking similar thoughts, which was easy to do when she was caught up in the haze that was Corbin.

Coming down from that high, she hit a harsh reality. A man was dead. She realized she'd been grabbing onto the first person she felt close to after hearing about Ed's murder. She couldn't help but think of a wife whose husband wouldn't come home. An icy chill raced down her spine.

Granted, she didn't like Ed personally. She didn't have to in order to hate the circumstances or feel awful this had happened.

"Hey," Corbin said, his tone full of compassion. "None of this is your fault."

"It sure feels like it sometimes," she admitted. She could go down the 'what if' path all day. What if she hadn't gone out with Kellan? What if she'd pushed him away instead like her instincts told her to? What if she'd stood her ground? What if she could go back and somehow fall out of love with Corbin? What if she'd been able to keep him in the friend zone?

He was one helluva friend, a good person to have on her side. In doing so, though, she was driving an even bigger wedge in Corbin's family.

"You couldn't have known any of this would happen. Life can be really unexpected at times and a whole lot random." His words soothed more of her soul than she should probably allow.

"I just need to get through tomorrow morning, and I'll be fine. I'll get back on the right track," she stated and immediately felt a chill in the air.

Corbin's blue eyes hardened and she hated that she'd hurt him.

It was necessary, though. They were falling into a well neither one would be able to climb out of and she would be placing him in an impossible position.

Plus, it was just a momentary temptation. The word, *just,* didn't come close to doing justice to what had happened between them a few minutes ago, but she had to think of it like that. She had to. She was stepping out of the Corbin vortex and back into the bitter cold reality. No matter how much she cared about him, and vice versa, any type of relationship between the two of them would drive an even bigger wedge in his family. He would be forced to choose between her and them.

And for what?

A relationship that might not even go the distance. Sure, they were great friends. Yes, they had incredible chemistry. But they weren't exactly talking marriage. Or anything even close for that matter. Would they have a few nights of hot sex and then realize they'd crossed another line? And then never be able to go back to civil conversation?

It was probably naïve of her to think there might come a time when they could actually be friends again.

"Sorry for practically attacking you," she finally said, breaking the awkward silence.

"Is that your version of what happened?" He was impossible to read behind the wall that had come up.

It hurt more than anything she'd ever experienced but was for the best.

"Last I checked, I was a willing participant," she said.

He stood there for a long moment, studying her. And then he folded his arms across a broad chest.

"You're right. Let's get through tonight. Shall we?" The ice in his voice stabbed her in the center of the chest.

"Okay, Corbin." She picked up her purse and walked into the kitchen, unable to look into those disappointed eyes a second longer.

11

Corbin watched Liv walk away from him. An annoying voice in the back of his mind told him to go after her. Tell her how much she meant to him and see if she felt the same way. He'd felt embers burning between them and it was stronger than anything he'd ever experienced. The kisses they'd shared were right up there with the best in his life. To be honest, they topped the list.

And then she'd just walked away like they'd been on the most amazing roller coaster for a few minutes and now the ride was over. The restraints lifted and they had to get out of the cart. She chose to run left without consulting him, knowing full well he was parked to the right.

So, yeah, he was nursing a bruised ego.

He chalked it up to bad timing. Wishing he could rewind the clock and tweak a few of his choices wouldn't do any good. Yet, there he was doing it anyway.

Get over it, Firebrand.

The intensity of what was happening between them was most likely due to a little thing called missed opportunity.

That, and the nature of the situation she faced. She was moving away from Lone Star Pass once she nailed the job interview, and she would. Staying here didn't seem like a good choice for her either. He could only imagine what the town would cook up for her if she dug her heels in. More smoke cans through the window?

Ed's murder changed the landscape of the case. Someone was now willing to kill in order to keep a secret.

Corbin's cell buzzed. He pulled it out and checked the screen. Lawler was calling. Liv would need to hear this, so he walked toward the kitchen as he answered the call.

"Mind if I put this on speaker?" he asked Lawler out of courtesy.

"I was going to suggest it," Lawler replied. "But I'm also going to ask both of you to sit down."

Corbin didn't meet Liv's eyes. He couldn't stand to see the hurt and fear there when he couldn't do anything about it. They took a pair of chairs on opposite sides of the table.

"Okay, we're sitting," he said.

"Corbin, your uncle, Keif, came forward to say he was behind the mystery offer for Liv's home," Lawler stated.

Liv gasped. She brought her hand up to cover her mouth. What else was he involved in? Her mind snapped to several possibilities, stopping on one.

"He denies having any involvement in Ed's death," Lawler clarified. "Says it's the reason he's making himself known. The investigation will tie him to Ed, and Keif wants to help because he says it would take up valuable time and the real perp might get away."

Corbin bit out a string of curses low and under his breath.

"Do you believe him?" he asked.

Liv had balled her fists and was staring out the window,

her gaze unfocused like she was looking inside herself. Was she trying to piece together why and how any of this could have happened?

His chest squeezed as anger burned at the thought of how his uncle had been the one pulling the strings, pressuring her to move.

"You know I can't comment further on an ongoing murder investigation," Lawler stated. "Suffice it to say he's being brought in for questioning."

"Can we watch?" Corbin didn't figure Lawler would agree but there was no harm in asking.

"I'm sorry, but that's not a good idea." Lawler's choice of words was interesting. It meant that technically they could come listen but he wasn't going to allow it. He must realize Corbin might have a difficult time controlling his temper.

"Is there any chance Ed was murdered to make Uncle Keif look like the good guy?" Corbin asked.

"How so?" Lawler's curiosity sounded piqued.

"Ed was about to reveal my uncle, which would be far more damning than in Uncle Keif came forward on his own," Corbin reasoned. His thoughts snapped to Kellan. He might have been involved and tried to save his father's name by getting rid of the one person who could implicate him. Kellan was a class-A jerk. He was clearly hurting over the divorce, and who wouldn't be considering he was losing the best thing that had ever happened to him in Liv. But a murderer?

Corbin didn't want to believe the possibility existed and he didn't want to be having this conversation about any member of his family.

"Agreed, and my office will be looking into all other possibilities as well," Lawler said, and his tone was all business now. "I'm sorry to have to be the one to bring this news to you, Corbin. I know how complicated this situation is for everyone involved."

"I appreciate the call, Sheriff," Corbin reassured. "And the heads-up."

The two exchanged goodbyes before ending the conversation.

"I knew they could be cruel, but this?" Liv's soft-spoken words threatened to pull him into the current again where all he could think about was how to take away her pain.

A little emotional distance would go a long way toward him living up to his promise of getting her through tomorrow morning, and then walking away.

"There are no words, Liv," he began, searching for a way to offer some kind of reassurance. Words seemed hollow and lacking. He reached over to cover her hand with his, and she drew her hand back like a snake bit it.

The move reminded him not to cross the line again. He was tempting fate and digging a deeper hole. His bruised ego took another hit, but it was for the best this way, he reasoned.

His heart had a mind of its own, refusing to listen to logic. Walking away, knowing it would likely be the last time he got to speak to Liv one-on-one threatened to shatter his heart. So, he had to find a way to stay tough.

There was no one else who had the power to make him feel that way. There was some good news in the realization because this feeling was for the birds. He never wanted to be in a position for someone to be able to gut him by pulling back her hand again.

"Why would he do this?" she finally asked, still staring out the window.

"The obvious answer is to push you out of town a little faster," he decided. "Kellan's father may have been doing all this without his knowledge. I certainly have questions of my own that I'd like answers to from my uncle."

"Kind of makes me want to dig my heels in and stay. Give the Paisleys a call and see if I can find a job right here in Lone Star Pass. Your mom made a good point about services like mine being needed here," Liv stated. It was good to see a little spark return to her eyes. Digging her heels in against his family could be a mistake. And yet, he wanted her to do it anyway.

"I wouldn't blame you for wanting to stick it to my uncle," he said.

"And Kellan," she quickly added. "He's trying to get back at me by erasing me altogether."

"Kellan was here this morning around the same time as Ed," Corbin pointed out. "Lawler won't know what kind of gun was used until he gets a report on ballistics. I'm not ready to tie Kellan to this crime yet."

"Which reminds me. Would he be stupid enough to use his own weapon?" she asked.

"To be clear, my cousin is a moron. I'll never know how he let you slip through his fingers, but I'm not convinced he's capable of murder. I saw the hurt in his eyes but this is too far out there." Corbin could see Kellan doing a whole lot of things, but this? There was no way in his mind that his uncle or cousin could be capable of such a heinous act.

She issued a sharp sigh.

"Then who?" she asked. "Because I don't want to believe it either."

"That's the question of the day," Corbin said. "Fingers do point at them."

"I wish the sheriff would have agreed to let us watch the interview," she said, flexing her fingers like she was trying to release tension.

"There's no way he's letting me in the same building as my uncle right now." Corbin hadn't exactly been secretive about needing to protect Liv. And the sheriff was right. Corbin would lose his cool at this point and that would do more harm than good.

"I can't imagine he wants me in there either," she said. She was right.

"Your presence might complicate the investigation," he agreed.

She gasped. "Do you think there's the slightest chance your uncle is responsible for what happened this morning?"

"Now that's a possibility whether directly or indirectly," he said. "Problem is I'm not sure which one applies, and I don't know him well enough to lean one way or the other."

THE THOUGHT SOMEONE hated Liv enough to sneak around and try to push her out of town didn't sit well. The fact someone involved had been murdered was almost incomprehensible. Reality was starting to sink in, and Liv was filled with sadness for the loss of life and for Ed's family.

For the time being, she had to find a way to set her emotions aside and focus on the case.

"If all this," she waved her hands in the air, "harassment was meant to force my hand a little sooner, why did Ed have to die?"

"Conspiracy comes to mind. I immediately snapped to someone trying to set up Uncle Keif," he said. "Someone who either knows about his plan or figured it out."

"Not your father...right?" She didn't want to believe brothers could be so cruel.

"Good point and, no, but this is going to be a hornet's

nest of accusations if the case isn't resolved quickly." Corbin held up his phone. "I gave up on trying to keep up with text messages from both sides of the family. My phone has been blowing up ever since the sheriff's call informing us of Ed's murder."

An icy shiver raced down her spine at hearing those words again, spoken out loud. Her mind didn't want to accept the news as truth. Every time she heard it repeated, it became a little more real to her and her heart broke a little more for Ed's family.

"Me being at the center of a Firebrand family feud isn't going to help my standing in this community." She wasn't feeling sorry for herself, only pointing out the obvious and how much more difficult it might be to stay if she chose to ride out the storm, pick up the pieces, and move on with her life here in Lone Star Pass.

"Which means if this morning's crime was a random person acting out, it could get worse," he stated. "There could be others."

"Your uncle hasn't exactly contacted me to apologize. Not that I'd be willing to speak to him after what he did. And, besides, even if he's not directly responsible for Ed's death, the man's blood is on Keifer Firebrand's hands for involving him," she stated.

"I couldn't agree more," Corbin said. He clenched his back teeth, a sign he was struggling to maintain an even temperament.

His cell buzzed and so did hers. Panic roared through her that there could be more bad news. He checked his screen and shook his head. "It's not the sheriff. It's my father."

Shock of all shocks, Liv tried to reel in her questions.

Corbin answered. She noted how formal he was with his

father. He repeated "Yes, sir," more than a few times before ending the call.

"What was that about?" she immediately asked, thinking she could use a cup of coffee about now. She glanced at the clock and saw the day had basically evaporated. If she was going to get up early, she needed to start thinking about winding down for bed.

"He called to insist he had no idea what was going on and has no involvement whatsoever," Corbin said. "He also sent his sympathy to you."

She studied him. His grip on the phone was so tight his knuckles were white. His tension levels were practically through the roof despite a calm exterior.

"Do you believe him?" she asked, wanting to know his opinion. Despite the divide between them, she did care about what he thought more than she wanted to admit for the time being. Corbin was intelligent and saw things others missed.

"This is the second time the man has called me in two days. I can count on one hand the number of times he's used one of these to contact me in the past decade." He held up his phone. "I'm inclined to believe he cares about what's happening and not because he's looking to save his own hide."

"I really hope for his sake he isn't. And he's a jerk for not calling you sooner." She'd seen firsthand how much Corbin had been hurt by his dad's actions when they were younger. The guy she knew wouldn't feel sorry for himself over it. And yet, the snub still broke her heart.

Brodie Firebrand wasn't the warm-and-fuzzy type. She got it. He'd never acknowledged her, despite all the hours she spent hanging around his ranch. He would pass right by without so much as a word. She was a stranger to him, so it didn't hurt her feelings. But his kids? He may not have been built for hugs and warmth, but that in no way excused him for missing every birthday dinner and sporting event of his sons. Corbin had played varsity baseball as a freshman. He had a solid arm, which also proved effective on the football field. Friday night lights had been a big part of their young lives. His dad wouldn't know what position Corbin played. Or probably any of his sons for that matter.

"The question is who would benefit from framing my family?" Corbin said after a thoughtful pause.

"Or hurting me," she stated. "Your family might have been caught in the crossfire."

"Which doesn't defend their actions. Their part in this is inexcusable," Corbin said.

She wouldn't argue there.

"We don't know their exact involvement at this point," she stated. "It's unfortunate their names came up at all."

The clock on the wall read seven o'clock. Exhaustion was settling into her bones, weighing down her limbs. "We should probably eat dinner and then go to bed."

She caught how that might sound and her cheeks flames.

"I didn't mean it to sound like..."

Corbin stood up with a smirk. She could have sworn she heard him say, *too bad.*

Granted, the kisses they'd shared in high school had imprinted her heart and invaded her thoughts—thoughts she didn't generally have a difficult time controlling. But this was Corbin and those kisses were probably made better by the fact they'd been cooking up in her memory for more than a decade. Like a stock that had been simmering so long the ingredients melded together creating the perfect spice blend.

And that was exactly what the kisses were...perfect. There were other 'P' words that came to mind. Potent. Passionate. There'd been so much heat she feared she'd burn from the inside out if they kept going, and yet the urgency building inside her made it impossible to stop. She'd wanted more and felt no shame in taking it. She had no doubt they would be even better now.

Corbin was perfection. For his sake, she could only pray his uncle was telling the truth. Kellan had made no secret out of the fact he couldn't stand her when she told him it was over. She'd probably hurt his ego more than anything else, but she really did feel truly felt awful for realizing she didn't love him, and never would. He would never be Corbin and that wasn't Kellan's fault. The perfect person was waiting for him out there, somewhere. She'd told him so straight out, which only proved to make matters worse.

Then, he'd called her out for being in love with Corbin. She'd denied it, of course, going with the whole, "It's me and not you," speech. It was true, though. She was the one who was broken and couldn't bring herself to love an otherwise perfectly good person. There was something wrong with her and now, looking at Corbin as he fixed a cup of coffee, she knew exactly what it was. No one could fill the void after losing their friendship.

Plus, Kellan had brought on all the charm when they went out. But after their marriage he'd turned into a jerk when he didn't get his way.

Someone needed to tell him that she wasn't a prize to be won. And the heart wanted what it wanted. She was relieved she'd seen Kellan's true colors quickly after they'd separated. Guilt might have convinced her to give their relationship a second chance.

Her only regret was agreeing to a relationship when

she'd been so devastated she could scarcely breathe. Lesson learned. And now the whole nightmare was about to end, and she...

The paperwork. She needed to sign the divorce decree. Would that make the nightmare go away?

"Any chance you have a lawyer who could review my divorce papers right now?"

12

Liv shouldn't be divorcing Kellan to Corbin's thinking. To be clear, it's not that he wanted her to stay married to his cousin, but rather that she never should have married him in the first place. And yet a piece of Corbin blamed himself for letting it happen. He was beginning to see just how much she'd been in mourning and how much that likely clouded her judgment two years ago. Another stab of guilt pierced his chest that he wasn't there for her. The fact she'd pushed him away should have made him double down. Dani's pregnancy scam had distracted him and he'd let Liv down in the worst possible way.

"Can I ask a question?" Corbin probably shouldn't go down this road, but he needed an answer.

"You can ask anything you want but that doesn't mean I'll answer." She shrugged non-committal and refused to look at him. It had been a long day. Her shoulders slumped forward and she exhaled like she needed a minute.

"Never mind," he said, realizing she didn't need him rubbing salt in that wound. There was no going back to change the past now, so what was the use in talking about why she'd turned her back on him and married Kellan? "You're tired and need a good night of sleep."

She nodded, pushing off the table to stand. "It has been a day. All I want right now is a shower, food, and a bed. Not necessarily in that order."

"I'll heat up some of Mom's leftovers and bring them upstairs if you want," he said.

"You would do that for me?" She cocked an eyebrow.

"Yes," he said, thinking he'd do just about anything for her.

"Give me fifteen minutes." She stifled a yawn before heading into the adjacent room. "I just need to check my phone first."

When he didn't hear the stairs creak a minute later, he joined her.

"What is it?" he asked.

She was staring at the cell, scrolling with her thumb.

"No more threatening messages from Kellan but I have eight calls from a number that I don't recognize and I'm trying to figure out who it is, in case it's related to my interview tomorrow morning," she stated.

One glance at the phone was all it took for him to be able to tell her. "That's my uncle's number."

She tossed the phone like she couldn't get it out of her hand fast enough. It landed on the sofa and bounced.

"I have nothing to say to him." She took a step back. "He never once spoke to me the whole time I was on the ranch. He barely said two words to me on my..." She flashed eyes at him and seemed to think better of continuing.

An alarm split the air.

"My truck." Corbin exploded out of the room but stopped the minute he stepped onto the front porch. He pulled his key fob from his front pocket and disarmed the alarm. The truck silenced immediately. There were no wild animals that he could see, and he wasn't parked underneath a tree. There was nothing visible that would cause his alarm to go off. The most probable scenario was that a person was out there attempting to...what...damage his truck?

Did this person believe Corbin would come running out, leaving Liv exposed?

Anger shot through him as he surveyed the yard, the nearby trees, and the lane. There was no sign of movement. Not so much as a rustle in the trees. Was this a setup to get him outside? Or another prank?

"Pack a bag," he said to Liv as he took a step backward into the house. He closed and locked the door before moving to the window.

"Why?" Liv was already there, surveying the area.

"I want to take you to the ranch," he said, "and before you refuse, hear me out."

"Go ahead." She folded her arms. With her chin up in defiance, she searched for any signs of a person outside.

"There's security at the ranch and I'll be able to keep you safe there, for one," he stated but he could already tell this was a losing battle.

"I can't set foot on Firebrand property, Corbin. That would only make my life worse which, if you hadn't noticed, isn't all that great right now," she admitted. "But that's not the reason. I can't leave here. They'll tear the place apart if I'm not here to defend it."

"We're leaving in the morning anyway. What's the harm in taking off a few hours early?" he asked.

"No, we're not." She shook her head. "The counseling center left a message. I'm not welcome there." She turned her face toward him. "And just who do you think is responsible for that?"

"I'm guessing my uncle, because I know Kellan doesn't have that kind of influence," he stated.

"Turns out they got a new donor who wants to go in a different direction," she said. "How did he even know?"

"Uncle Keifer has a whole lot of connections all over Texas," Corbin said. As he watched out the window, a truck pulled in and parked alongside Corbin's.

Brax stepped out of the driver's side and Corbin moved to the porch, scanning the area for any threat.

"Hustle up," Corbin waved at his brother.

Brax seemed to pick up on the stress of the situation. He picked up the pace. With one look, he got it. His chin went up and he glanced from side to side as he hopped onto the porch.

Corbin checked one more time before closing the door behind them both.

"What else happened?" Brax asked.

"My truck alarm just went off for no good reason." Again, it might have been a lure, but he wasn't taking the bait.

"When? Right now?" Brax moved to the window.

It seemed to dawn on all three of them at the same time.

"I scared them away," Brax stated.

"It's possible," Corbin said.

"What are you still doing here?" Brax asked.

"I was just asking Liv to come to the ranch with me, but she made a good point. Leave here and someone could destroy the place," Corbin supplied. He hated the way she stood there, arms crossed over her chest, looking like she'd run out of rope to hang onto.

"Then, I'm staying," Brax said, leaving no room for

doubt. "My wife is on the road and I'm not due to join her until the middle of the week. I'd be in the way at the ranch anyway."

Most of that was probably true.

"What about the job interview tomorrow?" Brax asked.

Corbin shook his head.

"It doesn't exist anymore," Liv said quietly. He'd misread her a few minutes ago. It wasn't defeat in her voice. She always got quiet when she was studying all angles of a situation. She was deep in thought, analyzing.

"How did that happen?" Brax asked.

"Our uncle became a donor," Corbin answered.

"I thought he wanted her out of town and away from Lone Star Pass." Brax's eyebrow drew together.

"I'm pretty sure he just wants me destroyed at this point," she said.

"You heard that he's the mystery man behind—"

Brax compressed his lips and shook his head. "That son-of-a—"

"Yes, he is," Corbin agreed.

Liv turned to face them. "If I have no job options, it looks like I'm digging my heels in and sticking around Lone Star Pass."

"You don't have to decide anything tonight," Corbin stated, despite the fact his heart just galloped at hearing the news. She might change her mind when she had a chance to reevaluate and rest. And he couldn't afford hope.

Liv was grown up enough to admit she'd made mistakes. Big ones. Was this the punishment?

Looking from Corbin to Brax and back, she couldn't

allow herself to think that way. Having them step up to have her back warmed her heart more than she could ever repay.

"Thank you both," she said. A surprising tear sprang to her eye. She blinked before it could make friends. "I'm not sure what I would do without you and your family."

"It's what we do for each other," Corbin said without hesitation and Brax agreed. While this kind of treatment might be normal for the two of them, she'd never experienced having a big family around. Her mother had been a single parent, one who'd loved Liv to the moon and back. Her sudden death two years ago had nearly broken Liv. She'd had a happy childhood despite her mother's long hours. If anyone thought teaching school was a nine to five job they were severely misinformed. Thinking about her mother meant one thing. She was spiraling. It was time to get some rest and reset the day tomorrow. She didn't have to get up early for an interview any longer but she did want a clear head so she could come up with names.

Signing those divorce papers jumped up on her priority list as well. She just needed to dig through them because complicated didn't begin to describe the language and the sheer amount of pages was daunting. The thing was bigger than *War and Peace.*

And then what? Maybe she could move on after breaking free from this area.

After all that had happened and was happening, why did the thought of leaving this town behind knock the wind out of her? She glanced at Corbin.

Because this was the only true home she'd ever known.

"I'm going to take that shower now," she said to the men who stood at the window in quiet conversation.

"I'll bring up food once you get settled," Corbin stated.

"Goodnight," Brax said and there was so much compassion in his voice. The two had been friendly growing up. She'd seen him around the ranch and at school. He'd always been nice to her but then she was almost always standing next to his brother.

"Night," she parroted before heading up. A long, hot bath sounded good about then, but she doubted she'd be able to keep her eyes open long enough. Nope, tonight, a shower would do the trick.

There was such a sense of comfort having Corbin and his brother downstairs. She had a layer of protection between her and whoever was intent on making her life miserable. The thought one of the people who'd thrown a can inside the house or set off the truck alarm could have killed Ed sat heavy in her heart. Again, she had to work to set those feelings aside or threaten being sucked under and into the riptide. The best way she could help with the investigation was to keep a clear head.

Once inside the shower, she stood there a solid minute in the warm water. She wished she knew how Corbin's uncle's interview went at the sheriff's office. Was he being held in the jail?

Technically, he'd gone in to speak with Sheriff Lawler voluntarily. Did that mean Keif was a witness or a suspect?

A few minutes later, she was showered, dressed in pajamas, and sitting up in bed. She decided to turn her phone off for the night, figuring she'd heard enough bad news for one day. Besides, the only person she wanted to speak to for the rest of the evening was the man coming up the stairs.

The wood flooring in the hallway creaked and groaned underneath Corbin's feet before his tall, masculine frame filled the doorway.

"The windows and fans worked," he said, stepping

inside with a tray in his hands. "I can hardly smell the smoke in here anymore."

He walked over and then sat on the side of the bed. The mattress dipped underneath his weight. He reached over her with the tray and set it on her right side. Her stomach free fell with him this close, so close she could breathe in his spicy, masculine scent.

"Or we might be getting used to it," she admitted, needing to speak before she got lost in the haze that was Corbin.

"Probably both are true," he stated with a smile before motioning toward the tray. "Mom's meatballs."

"Legendary," she agreed. She hadn't tasted those in a solid two years. Her mouth watered, despite her somber mood.

"We never really talked about her," Corbin said and, somehow, she didn't think they were still talking about *his* mother.

The minute she looked up at him, she knew exactly who he was talking about. She shook her head because she fully understood who he meant. And, no, they hadn't.

"I don't talk about her with anyone," she said by way of explanation, realizing how much it hurt just to bring her up in conversation. There'd been no one to talk to in the two years since Dani had made it clear leaning on Corbin wasn't an option. A deep well of sadness threatened to empty Liv from the inside out at remembering how awful her mother's accident had been. How much she'd wanted to lean on Corbin. And how impossible and unfair that would have been to him in his new life—a life that would be centered around Dani and not Liv. Hot tears burned the backs of her eyes and she struggled to keep them at bay.

"It's okay to cry," Corbin soothed.

"I'm not a crier, Corbin," she quickly defended, figuring he didn't know the half of why she was about to lose it. Knowing it was probably better if he didn't. "You know me."

"You're the strongest person I know, Liv." He reached out and clasped their hands. Contact sent warmth rushing through her and unleashed a few of those tears.

"I don't want to cry," she warned.

"I'm not asking you to," he said, and his voice was filled with compassion—compassion she hadn't experienced in two years until now. Compassion that threatened to lower her defenses as she realized she'd been bottling everything up. No wonder she'd felt so alone. She'd cut herself off from the few people who were important to her, namely Corbin's side of the family.

In losing her mother, she'd lost what little family she had. Losing Corbin at the same time had caused her to lose everything all at once. Had she buried her feelings so deep they'd never surface again? Had she shut off the valve in order to survive?

Using his thumb, he drew circles in the palm of her hand, causing all kinds of warmth to flood her senses.

"Corbin, don't." Her protest sounded weak, even to her.

"I'm here, Liv. I should have been here for you a long time ago. I'm late to the game and I'll never be able to apologize enough for my mistakes or make any of it up to you." His words, his voice, were balm to a wounded soul.

And yet, letting him inside her heart now would lead to what? More pain when he moved on with his life after this ordeal was over?

"I just can't go there right now," she warned, knowing full well she would never be able to recover if she let him in again.

"Right now, or ever?" His question threatened to bust up

more of her resolve—resolve that was weakening by the second.

"Ever." She shot a look at him. "That's what I should say."

"What do you *want?*" His question wasn't helping keep her emotions in check.

"Things I can't have," she said low and under her breath.

"What does that mean, Liv?"

She wanted to tell him, to be honest with him about the way she felt. What good would that do?

13

"We sure did one helluva job *not* ruining our friendship," Liv said with a half-smile, and Corbin realized how quickly she was diverting the conversation away from the topic of her mother.

"I'm here for you no matter what or who you want to talk about. If you want to joke around, I'm around for that too." He caught her gaze and held it. There was so much sadness behind those beautiful brown eyes. "But I don't think you're talking about the important stuff with anyone else now and haven't in the past. Keeping it bottled up inside will only hurt more down the road. I wouldn't be a real friend if I didn't notice or warn you."

"Real friends have been in short supply in my life recently," she stated.

"And why is that?" he asked. "I just assumed you pushed me away because you'd fallen for him." He couldn't bring himself to say his cousin's name.

"Is that what you think?" She seemed downright shocked.

"It was," he admitted. "I didn't have any evidence to the contrary."

"I lost one of the most important people in my life, Corbin. I didn't know which way to turn," she stated. The look in her eyes said they'd only scratched the surface of why. There was a mix of hurt and regret embedded so deep she'd become an expert at glossing over them.

"It has taken me way too long to say this, but I'm here now, Liv." His comment was met with a look of disbelief.

"But for how long?" she asked quietly.

She would ask the one question he didn't have an answer to. His heart said forever but he couldn't and wouldn't make a promise he wasn't one hundred percent certain he could keep.

"Talk to me about her," he said, dodging the question and hoping she would let it slide.

Liv exhaled sharply. She dropped her gaze to the blanket and started toying with the edge.

He reached over to her, gently placing his finger underneath her chin to lift her face toward him.

"Hey. It's okay. I'm right here," he repeated as their gazes met. His heart took a hit staring into those brown eyes of hers.

"It's hard, Corbin," she said and there was so much bravery in her voice.

"I know," he said, dropping his hand to meet hers.

"She was my world growing up, and I don't even know if I told her how important she was to me." Her chin quivered and a few tears rolled down her cheeks.

"The feeling was mutual," he reminded. "It was so easy to tell in the way she looked at you in class or at home."

"Yeah?" Her voice trembled.

"She loved you, Liv. You were everything to her," he said.

All she needed was a reminder of how close the two of them had been.

"Who was the first person you wanted to call when you got into UT?" he asked.

"My mom," she said. "Because you were already standing next to me."

"I happened to be at your house when you opened up the e-mail," he pointed out. "You would have called me second."

She shook her head. "I would have called you first."

"I highly doubt it," he countered.

"Not because I didn't love my mother." She cocked her head to one side. "The other day, you said something about taking the ones you love for granted. That describes my relationship with my mother to a T. I took her for granted and now she's gone and I can't tell her how important she was to me and I can't hug her anymore..."

A sob escaped. He leaned in and looped his arms around her. She scooted toward him and buried her face in his chest. He whispered reassurances into her ear as she let go of all the pent-up emotion while in his arms.

Corbin had no idea how long the two of them sat there. He didn't care either. The sun descended as he consoled her, offering all the comfort he could while hoping it was making a difference in some small way. Liv deserved the world and part of him wished he was the one who could give it to her.

"I'm sorry," she whispered.

"Don't be," he said. "You haven't done anything wrong."

"I just wish I could tell my mom how I feel about her. The way we left things feels so unfinished," she stated.

"Do you want to go there?" He referred to her mother's burial site.

"I haven't been there since..." She got quiet and he knew she meant since the funeral.

"We can go anytime you want," he said, stroking her hair. "I'll take you myself."

"The thing is...she's not there anymore," she said. "It's just a piece of stone placed in memory of her."

Corbin realized that was true, but it also gave people a place to go. But Liv was right. Her mother wasn't in a graveyard. There was one place he could think of where her mother's spirit would be.

"I know where to go," he said.

"Oh yeah?" She looked at him with red, puffy eyes and still managed to be the most beautiful woman he'd ever seen.

"It's where her heart was when she wasn't with her daughter," he reassured. "Are you still hungry? Because it'll wait until after you eat."

"As a matter of fact, I'm starved. I feel like I can truly eat for the first time in a very long time," she admitted, polishing off the meatball sandwich. There was a lightness to her now that he hadn't seen in far too long.

"I'll wait downstairs," he said and heard the huskiness in his own voice. "That way, I can let Brax know the plan."

He started to get up but she tugged him back down again. Before he could protest, she threw her arms around his neck.

"Thank you, Corbin," she said. "Talking about her feels good and there's no one else who understands how much she meant to me than you. It's probably the reason I don't talk about her with anyone else. I just don't think they'd get it like you do. You know?"

Corbin nodded, and then he dipped his head, stopping himself before he pressed a kiss to her lips.

"I think I do know," he said when he pulled back because she was the first person he wanted to call when great news hit and the first he wanted to reach out to when his day had tanked.

"It's good to talk," she said and her eyes were glittery with need—need he couldn't afford to think too much about when she was this vulnerable no matter how right it felt to claim those lips.

LIV CHANGED INTO STREET CLOTHES, and then stood at her dresser. Her mother had left behind a ladybug pin that had been worn by Liv's grandmother. The pin had been handed to Liv's mother after a rare bone disease claimed granny's life. Liv's mother explained it would one day belong to Liv. The pin was just this little thing, not much bigger than a tack, but it meant the world to Liv.

Until now, she hadn't been able to pull it out of the drawer, much less wear it. She pinned it on her shirt, wishing her mother was here to be the one to wear it.

Talking to Corbin had helped Liv realize she hadn't given herself permission to think about her mother in the past two years, let alone mourn her. Skye Holden had the most amazing smile. Liv got her eyes from her mother, or so she'd been told but her mother's had always been somehow deeper, richer, more vibrant. She'd given up pretty much any sense of a social life to be there for Liv. Her mother was devoted to her students and loved her job. Teaching had been her calling, despite the relentless paperwork and long hours that came with the job. None of the burdens ever outweighed her passion for teaching.

While most complained about teenagers in general, Liv's mother had always said that that was the time kids started to become more interesting people. They could hold a real conversation, and their penchant for debating and questioning everything they'd ever known didn't bother her. She used to smile and say teenagers were meant to be curious about the world, after all, they were so close to the age where they would inherit it.

Tears streamed down Liv's face. Not tears from sadness but tears from the memories—and they were all good. If there was such a thing as saints on earth, Skye Holden would surely have qualified. Students loved her mother. She'd seen the tributes that had been placed on their walls on social media after the accident. Her mother had touched so many lives.

A sense of pride washed through Liv. She would always miss her mother and stopping to remember her somehow made her feel closer when all Liv expected to feel was the pain of losing her. She thought about all the pints of ice cream the two of them had shared on Friday night movie nights when they'd curl up in front of the TV to watch a show in their pajamas.

They might not have had everything, big house, expensive cars, and yet in many small ways, it felt like they did. They had each other. Beyond that, there was always food on the table and presents on holidays.

Liv felt a sense of shame for the high school years when she'd pushed her mother away, insisting she ride to school with Corbin when in truth she was embarrassed to show up with her mother. If she could take anything back...

Liv redeemed herself somewhat after going to college and realizing all the little things her mother did on a daily basis to make her life better. The care. The meals. The laundry.

When given a choice of all the degree plans she could have chosen, she'd followed in her mother's footsteps. Turned out, an English degree didn't do a whole lot of good unless she wanted to be a teacher where she'd worked at the same school as her mother. After the accident, Liv couldn't go back to the same high school she'd worked when her mother was alive. There were too many memories there. She'd stayed long enough for the principal, Mrs. Bench, to replace two teachers after the devastating crash.

The unfairness of her mother dying when she was still so young and in such a senseless manner struck like a physical blow. The other driver was cutting through Lone Star Pass to avoid highway traffic on her way north to Waco. She'd been too tired to be behind the wheel in the first place, had dozed off before crossing over and striking Liv's mother head-on.

Liv glanced down at the ladybug pin and smiled. Remembering dredged up old pain. But a warm feeling settled over her too. She freshened up in the mirror before hearing a vehicle approach. More of Corbin's family?

It wouldn't surprise her. The fact a couple of his brothers and his mother had stopped by earlier reminded her just how wonderful Corbin's side of the family was. Trust her when she said the other side wasn't nearly so kind. But then, they seemed to look at her as the enemy from day one and they were probably right in doing so.

"I wonder who that is," she heard Corbin say as she reached the bottom of the stairs.

"This isn't one of yours?" she asked.

Both Corbin and Brax shrugged.

"No one owns a white Suburban that I know of," Corbin said. He looked to his brother.

"I'm drawing a blank too," Brax said.

"Maybe you should stay inside while I investigate," Corbin said to her.

Recognition dawned.

"That's no buyer," she stated. "It's my Uncle Jody."

"Jody Reiss?" Brax asked.

"That's the one," she said.

"I heard he moved away from here a long time ago," Brax said. "Got into some trouble with the law in Galveston."

"He called out of the blue to offer support the other day." Liv sure didn't remember giving him an invitation. "He mentioned something about checking on me again. I thought he was talking about a phone call."

Uncle Jody climbed out of the driver's seat of his SUV. He stopped at the driver's door and she could see him reaching for something inside. He took a step back and closed the door. The object in his hand was a cane. He walked with a limp away from the older SUV, and seemed to rely heavily on the cane.

"I better go see what he wants," she said, thinking at least he didn't have a suitcase in the other hand.

"Mind if we join you?" Corbin asked and she could hear the protectiveness in his voice.

"I'll stay back," Brax said. "Mind if I put on a pot of coffee?"

"Help yourself," she said, figuring they were going to need it to get through this visit. Her short-lived second wind at the thought of going to her mother's favorite place waned at the sight of her uncle.

Shouldn't she be more excited about a visit from family?

Maybe, but she didn't know this man and he'd never

visited much at all while she was growing up. When he did, it seemed like her mother's nerves were set on edge.

Liv opened the door and Corbin reached over her head to hold it open. She led the way outside, and he was right behind her, reaching for her hand. With their fingers linked, she felt a whole lot better about facing Uncle Jody.

"Liv? Is that you?" The older man walked up to the porch, looking like it winded him to make the journey. "You're all grown up."

"Yes, I am." She smiled but it was one hundred percent awkward to be staring at this man in person. She should probably say it was good to see him. Instead, she went with, "What made you decide to visit?"

"Heard there's been a mess of trouble in town. Thought maybe you could use a little family support." Uncle Jody was younger than her mother, so he was probably in his early fifties. He could best be described as thick with big arms. At first glance, he looked like the kind of guy who'd be sitting on the porch on a sofa, throwing back beers all day. There was something about his smile that didn't sit well. She couldn't quite put her finger on why.

"That's really nice of you." She motioned toward Corbin with her free hand. "As you can see, I have friends here."

"Oh, well, I drove all this way for nothing then." He took a couple of steps toward the porch. "I'll just make the return trip to Corpus in the morning."

She didn't see how she could turn him away, especially considering it seemed to take great effort to walk from the SUV to the porch.

"Have you met my friend here?" She motioned toward Corbin.

"Corbin Firebrand." He stuck his hand out toward Uncle Jody

Uncle Jody's eyes widened when he heard the last name. He took the offering and shook. "Nice to meet you."

"I was just about to say the same thing," Corbin said, but his voice told another story and his expression said it all. Uncle Jody was up to something.

14

"Do you have an overnight bag I can get for you?" Corbin asked Liv's uncle. The man had ties to the community and his recent out-of-the-blue call followed by this visit wasn't sitting well. Not to mention in all the years he'd known Liv and her mother this uncle had rarely visited. On the rare chance he stopped by, Ms. Holden always seemed a little nervous about being alone in the house with him.

"There's one in the backseat if you don't mind." Jody fished out a key fob from his pocket and unlocked the vehicle.

"Not at all." Corbin walked over to the SUV as Liv ushered her uncle inside the house.

Corbin's main motivation for the offer was to see if there were any indicators of the real reason for Jody's visit. Was he there to spy for Uncle Keif? At this point, Corbin wasn't ruling anything out. The fact his uncle could have orchestrated the 'mystery' offer to buy out Liv in the first place was more than frustrating. A man had lost his life, presumably because of this deal.

Ed Roberts hadn't exactly been Corbin's favorite person, But he didn't trust this man as far as he could throw him. He opened the vehicle's door and reached for the bag. The inside smelled like greasy fries. Fast food wrappers littered the floorboard and Corbin had half a mind to grab a pair of gloves from his truck so he didn't have to touch anything. Plus, the sheriff could probably lift fingerprints from the handle.

Then again, the same could be said for the wheel and anything Jody touched while inside the home. So, Corbin decided to let it go and move on. He glanced at the front seat. On the passenger side, there were more wrappers and not much else unless something was buried underneath.

Corbin wouldn't mind cracking open the suitcase but couldn't risk being gone much longer or getting caught. If Uncle Jody was up to something and he suspected Corbin was onto him, the guy wouldn't relax. He'd be more careful. Make fewer mistakes.

If there was a connection between Jody and Corbin's family, he intended to find out. Corbin pulled his cell phone out of his back pocket and fired off a text to alert the sheriff to Jody's arrival. He followed up asking if the sheriff knew where Jody lived and what his story was.

Lawler responded that he'd check into it.

Satisfied that he'd done as much as he could for the time being, he picked up the suitcase and headed inside. The trip he originally thought he'd be taking Liv on tonight to her mother's former classroom and then the quarry would have to wait. His chest swelled with pride that Liv had opened up to him about missing her mother.

He wasn't there for her two years ago in the way he should have been. It wasn't too late to step up now.

Corbin headed inside and set the suitcase down beside the door.

"Hope that wasn't too much trouble," Jody said. He seemed pretty comfortable sitting in a lounger in the living room. Was it an act?

"I was just asking my uncle what he's been up to the past few years," Liv informed and her smile was strained. "Turns out, he's been working a fishing boat in Galveston until he recently took a fall and rolled his ankle."

"Doctor said it should be fine in a few weeks," Jody said, waving it off.

Brax shot a look of distrust that Jody didn't seem to pick up on. Corbin felt the same way. He wouldn't believe a word that came out of this man's mouth.

"And what brings you here?" Corbin asked, figuring he might get a different answer than Liv did a few minutes ago. Asking the same question from a different source or in a different way was something he'd observed Lawler do during recent investigations.

"My niece." He didn't miss a beat. "My friends reached out to say she's being given a hard time and I couldn't sit by and do nothing."

"Nice of you to drop everything for her," Corbin said doing his best to sound like he admired the effort. He'd never been a good liar, mostly because he wasn't practiced at it. He needed to be convincing with Jody, though. This seemed like a good time to remind himself of the stakes. Liv's life could be on the line.

Now that her interview had been canceled, she needed to come up with a new plan. The thought that she might stick around in Lone Star Pass lit a dozen campfires inside him. He had every intention of making certain she'd be safe if that turned out to be the call for her. He wasn't quite ready to admit how much he wanted her to make the choice but it was like a tsunami building inside him.

Once the immediate threat was over, his next step would be to find a way to make her feel safe again in the town where she grew up. Was that even possible at this point? Her trust had been broken. Folks might still be rude to her and give her the cold shoulder, both of which were unacceptable. And then there was Kellan. He might continue to do everything in his power to make her life miserable. Corbin being here was making it worse for her. The wedge between the family was a cavern at this point.

The sound of another vehicle coming up the lane caused four heads to turn toward the noise.

"I'll see who it is," Corbin offered.

"The coffee is probably ready. Who's in for a cup?" Brax asked, his presence combined with Corbin's seemed to set Jody on edge as the man's gaze bounced between the two of them regularly since Corbin entered the room. *Good.*

LIV'S HEART skipped a few beats when she heard the vehicle outside. Her nerves were a little too on the edge, no doubt part of the fallout from the last couple of days. She would be unpacking all that had happened for months down the line but right now she needed to focus on finding out who was after her and why.

She reminded herself that her recent 'visitors' for lack of a better term didn't exactly announce their arrival. She looked to Brax as he returned. "Could this be more of the cavalry?"

"No one told me they were coming," he admitted. He balanced four mugs of coffee, two handles in each hand. He set all four down on the coffee table before passing each one out.

"Mr. and Mrs. Paisley?" Corbin said, sounding as shocked as she felt.

Liv hopped up and headed toward the door. Corbin was a step behind. She glanced at Brax at the last minute and gave him a look she hoped he could interpret. He responded with a slight nod indicating he would keep an eye on her uncle.

"So, what kind of work did you say you do?" Brax asked Jody.

"I've been working a fishing boat," Jody responded as she slipped out the door.

Tension sent her pulse through the roof as the Paisleys exited their vehicle. Mr. Paisley left their car running as his wife reached into the backseat and produced a basket. She walked straight to Liv. Mrs. Paisley was on the short side. She had the kind of soft middle that said she was probably an amazing baker, or at least one who liked to sample her product. Other than that, she had an oval-shaped face and a warm smile. Her hair was graying, and she had to be in her early sixties. It dawned on Liv that she'd been a kindergarten teacher years ago, before retiring early to travel with her husband once her children were grown.

"I apologize for not coming around before now and I know it's getting late," Mrs. Paisley began. She held out the picnic basket. "I made bread and muffins. These were some of your mom's favorites and I thought you might like to have them."

Her husband was just shy of six-feet-tall with a balding head and a serious face. His middle section looked like he enjoyed his wife's baking too.

"Thank you," Liv said, taking the offering.

The Paisleys greeted Corbin and wished his mother well. Did Lucia Firebrand have anything to do with this?

"This is really nice of you," Liv stated, still trying to figure out why they'd stopped by today of all days.

Mr. Paisley seemed content to step back while his wife took the lead, but his show of support warmed Liv's heart.

"It's nothing and has been a long time coming, if you ask me," Mrs. Paisley said. "I'm just glad you're back and I hope you'll consider staying around. We need more good people in this town."

"I don't know what to say." Liv rarely ever found herself in the position to be speechless. The kindness caused her eyes to well up with tears. "I'll start with thank you."

She walked to Mrs. Paisley and gave her a hug. The older woman's embrace brought more of those tears to life. Thankfully, she didn't soak Mrs. Paisley's dress with them.

"You're not alone any longer, sweetie," Mrs. Paisley whispered, her voice hitched on the words. "Your mom was one my favorite people in the world. I won't fail her again."

"Thank you isn't nearly big enough to cover how wonderful you've been," she said to both of the Paisleys. "This means so very much."

As Liv stumbled over her words, overwhelmed with emotion, another vehicle drove up the lane.

"Reach out if you need anything." Mrs. Paisley patted Liv's hand.

"I will do that," Liv promised. The smell of fresh bread wafting in the evening breeze caused her stomach to growl.

"We best be on our way," Mrs. Paisley stated with a smile that hinted something was up. She nodded toward Corbin. "Your mother has my number. Would you see to it that Liv programs it into her phone?"

"Yes, ma'am." Corbin saluted and smiled.

As the Paisleys pulled away, another vehicle parked. The McDermotts stepped out of their truck. They were a sweet couple close in age with the Paisleys. Mrs. McDermott used to teach middle school around the same time Mrs. Paisley taught kindergarten. Was the teacher connection a coincidence?

Mrs. McDermott hopped out of the passenger side of the family's truck. She wore a bright smile as she carried a tin in her hands.

"Was that Rita in the car pulling away?" Mrs. McDermott asked with a wink after acknowledging Corbin.

"Yes," Liv responded but she'd never called Mrs. Paisley by her first name.

"I was hoping to beat her over here," Mrs. McDermott stated. Go figure. Teachers could be competitive with each other. She laughed. "Looks like I'll have to take the silver medal on this one."

She held out the tin.

"These are my famous snickerdoodles," she said proudly.

"I've heard about these." This really took Liv back years ago to when she taught. Mrs. McDermott's snickerdoodles were the stuff of legend.

"I made 'em special for you." She beamed. "Harold is still grumbling because I wouldn't let him touch his until we delivered yours."

Harold stood in the background and waved. Arms full, Liv did her best to return the gesture.

"I was real sorry to hear about your beautiful mama," Mrs. McDermott said. "We were all so devastated we didn't know what to do." She wiped a stray tear. "We've pulled our act together now, though. We're here for you, hon." She looked at Corbin and held his gaze. "Put my number in her cell right now, please."

"Can I put it in mine if I promise to transfer it the minute she sets these gifts down?" he asked with a smile as he motioned toward Liv as she struggled to figure out a way to get hers out of her pocket.

Mrs. McDermott practically cackled.

"Of course," she said. She rattled off her number before glancing at the white SUV and lowering her voice. "What's he doing here?"

"You know what my uncle drives?" Liv asked.

"Afraid so," she stated making a tsk-tsk sound. "Check the miles on it. They're probably lower than they should be, which is what happens when you've been in the slammer for the past two years."

"Wait...what?" Liv asked. She heard the first time but she needed a repeat so it could absorb.

Mrs. McDermott leaned in, "Word has it that he stole from the last boat captain he worked for. He did time for it and has been unofficially 'banned' from ever working in Galveston again."

"That's good to know." Something niggled at the back of her mind about Uncle Jody, but she couldn't quite put a finger on what it was. Her head was still spinning from the generosity of neighbors and her heart was full. She was realizing just how much she'd shut herself off from everyone and everything after her mother's death. Looking back, Kellan's place had been a good place to hide from the world.

One thing was certain, Uncle Jody needed to go. It was highly possible he'd only shown up to get a free ride.

"Call me if you need anything," Mrs. McDermott said before bringing Liv into another hug. She pulled back and said, "Even if you just need someone to talk to."

"I will," Liv promised.

As Mrs. McDermott climbed inside her vehicle, another made its way up the lane. Liv noticed a pattern as another former teacher parked and then approached with a food offering.

"This was your mother's favorite dish when I brought it to potlucks," Ms. Abernathy said. The ninth-grade math teacher had been one of Liv's favorites. Tall with long hair that was always in a loose bun on top of her head, she had a certain natural elegance with the way she carried herself. When she was younger, she probably could have pulled off being a runway model with her looks, but teaching had been her calling. She was aging with grace and Liv doubted a catwalk would ever put the spark in Ms. Abernathy's eye that she'd witnessed when a student had a lightbulb moment in her classroom.

"I remember this. Mom always talked about your Shrimp Chowder with Herb Drop Biscuits. Said the shrimp was always so fresh because you met it at the boat." The memory brought another smile to her face. The smell said she was in for a real treat. She had no idea what she would do with all this food. Maybe she could freeze some of it. Then again, Corbin and Brax could probably help put some of it away tonight.

Ms. Abernathy gave her phone number to Corbin before retreating to her vehicle. Three additional vehicles followed in succession and Liv knew one thing for certain...she would never be alone again.

"See. Not everyone in Lone Star Pass is a jerk," Corbin said as the last vehicle disappeared down the lane. "I got a text from my mom saying this was only the beginning. The minute she put out word you weren't being treated well, an army jumped to your defense."

"Remind me to thank her," she said, not that she would need it. What she meant to say was she needed to find a way to thank his mother enough.

"Will do," Corbin said before balancing a couple of dishes on his arm while fishing out his cell phone. He held his cell in the air. "What do you say about finding a hotel room near the highway for your uncle?"

"I think that's the best for all involved," she agreed.

"Good. Then, this one is one me." Corbin made the call, booked the reservation, and then there was only one thing left to do...tell Uncle Jody.

15

Corbin followed Liv inside the house where Brax seemed to be in a staring contest with Jody. Liv's uncle definitely seemed to be uncomfortable, which didn't bother Corbin one bit. He helped Liv bring all the dishes and baskets into the kitchen.

"I've got these," he said to her. He nodded toward the living room. "Why don't you go in and deliver the good news."

Her lips compressed into a frown.

"As much as I want him gone, it's never easy to disappoint someone I barely know," she admitted.

"You got this, Liv." Corbin fought the temptation to dip his head and kiss her. He thought about feathering a kiss on the dimple before finding her lips with his. It was as though a bomb detonated in his chest just thinking about it. He couldn't continue going down that road because when he looked into her glittery eyes, he saw something that looked a whole lot like need.

"I got this," she said, shoulders back, looking more confident this time.

"And when you come back," he started, dropping his gaze to her lips, realizing he'd barely dodged a bullet but not yet ready to admit defeat. "I'd like to..."

He stopped himself right there. No use voicing his desire while he couldn't act on it. Instead, he shook his head.

"Then, this won't take long at all," she teased, and then wiggled an eyebrow, lightening the mood. Because a few moments ago, the air crackled with tension.

He couldn't hold back a smile.

"Besides, I've never been one for holding in a secret for long," she said.

"Do you want me in the room?" he asked.

"Nah. I'll be quick," she said. "No sense dragging it out."

Corbin moved to where he could hear as it went down.

"Thank you for stopping by the house tonight, Uncle Jody," Liv said to her uncle.

Brax appeared in the doorway almost immediately after she left, his coffee cup in hand. "Figured I'd get a refill and give the two of them some privacy."

"Seems like a pretty solid idea to me," Corbin admitted, going back to work across the room, filling the fridge.

"Do you know what she wants to talk to him about?" Brax asked.

"I booked a room for him near the highway." Corbin lowered his voice. "She wanted to be the one to tell him."

"Gotcha. Good idea," Brax stated. "I figured something was up and I didn't mind walking away since there isn't much he can do, considering his condition and the fact that we're literally in the next room," Brax said. "Not that she needs the help. Liv is a strong and capable person."

"Truer words have never been spoken," Corbin said. "It's just unfortunate how much the deck has been stacked against her, thanks to our jerk of a cousin."

"Has she said why she did it?" Brax had to be referring to marriage.

Corbin shook his head. It wasn't his place to talk about it either.

"About Kellan..." Brax's hesitation to continue raised the alarm for Corbin.

"Go ahead and say what's on your mind," Corbin urged.

"All I'm saying is that it's obvious to me and everyone else that you still have feelings for Liv," Brax admitted, pausing before continuing.

Corbin shot his brother a warning look.

"Look. It's pretty clear to anyone with eyes that the two of you feel the same way toward each other," Brax continued. "The past two years watching you be miserable, as your brother, has pretty much been awful. I know the situation has been complicated but not from my viewpoint and, I'm sure, anyone else's whose viewpoint really matters would feel the same way."

"Dad, for one," Corbin stated.

"When have you ever cared about what he thought?" Brax countered. His direct question definitely caught Corbin off guard a little bit.

"What are you saying?" Corbin rolled his shoulder to ease some of the tension building. "I may not be close with the man but I do respect him as being our father."

Brax shot Corbin a look and it dawned on him why. As the family had recently learned, Brax was blood, a Firebrand through and through. However, Lucia Firebrand was not his biological mother. In fact, their father had cheated on their mother while she was pregnant with Corbin. Brax's birth certificate had been fudged to make it seem like he was older than he was.

"Are you saying that you've lost all sense of respect for the man?" Corbin asked his brother.

"Our mother is one of the kindest, most amazing people God put on this earth. Our father cheated on her when they were young. Who knows what he's done since. He has never been close with any one of us. So, no, his opinion doesn't count a whole helluva lot in my book." Brax's set chin and determined gaze said he one hundred percent felt those words.

"You know how Mom feels and we all followed her lead," Corbin said.

"Doesn't dismiss what the man did," Brax argued.

"No. It doesn't. And the fact you came into this world by another mother doesn't make you any less our mother's son. We all agree," Corbin continued.

"You know I appreciate it. There's no question in my mind about how you guys have accepted me," Brax said. "He never apologized or acknowledged what he did. Not even to me. So, there it is. I don't respect the man who refuses to attempt to make it right."

"That's fair," Corbin said. "And there's no doubt you're my brother, through and through. I don't need a piece of paper to tell me what I already know.

Brax crossed the room and brought his brother into a bear hug. The family had become closer because of their dad's actions. Could Corbin act on his feelings toward Liv?

LIV CLOSED the front door after walking her uncle out to his SUV. She'd carried his overnight bag and placed it in his backseat. She overheard Brax and Corbin talking in the kitchen, so she made a beeline to join them. Walking in and catching them mid-bear hug warmed her heart.

She hadn't given a whole lot of thought to her future. The idea of having a family of her own was always 'someday' and not now. Here she was thirty-six-years old, almost single, and about to embark on a new chapter in her career, and in her life.

She cleared her throat to let the guys know she was in the room, not wanting to surprise them during a tender moment between brothers. Being an only child had its advantages and equal downsides. She'd never known what it was like to have a sibling who she could rely on and who always had her back. But then, not everyone got along with their family members in the way many of the Firebrands did. In fact, being around their family growing up was part of the reason she had a rare occasion of thinking she might like to have a family of her own.

"Hey. How did it go in there?" Corbin asked. His gaze bounced from the window and back to Liv.

"He was surprisingly good with it. I did my best to let him down easy by telling him that Brax needed a place to stay tonight and there just wasn't enough room for four people to be here and be comfortable. I told him that you felt bad about it, so you offered to cover his room for the night," she said.

"Sounds like he took it better than I expected him to," Corbin said. There was something in Jody's eyes that Corbin didn't trust. "I got a text from the sheriff. He's keeping Uncle Keif overnight."

"I think I know what you're about to say and I agree one hundred percent. I doubt he wanted me to have to bring in the big guns on this one." Her gaze bounced from Brax to

Corbin and they both chuckled, breaking up some of the tension of the day.

"Speaking of good fortune, I can't believe Mrs. McDermott brought over her snickerdoodles," she said.

"The smells in this kitchen are amazing," Brax stated. "Did I mention how well cookies go with a fresh cup of coffee?"

He made a show of topping off his mug.

"Make yourself at home," Liv said, waving her arm around like they were in a showroom and she was unveiling a new car. She had every intention of having one of those cookies. She walked over to the tin and opened the container. She passed cookies around before tossing one in her own mouth, realizing this must be what heaven was like. She blinked up at Corbin, and thought, *Correction, that's what heaven feels like.*

After they'd dipped into the treats, she realized it was getting pretty late. She'd bit back three yawns in the past five minutes and Corbin had called her on it. She was tired but it wasn't the same as earlier when she'd gone to bed. It had been heavy and she'd been cloaked in sadness last time. Now, there was so much more lightness surrounding her and for the first time in a while a real sense of hope that she might have a decent future here. In fact, one of the first calls she planned to make with the new phone numbers she had was to Mrs. Paisley, to talk to her about the possibility of a job. Funds were getting low and she needed to get out of the mess of the divorce, sign the papers, and put that huge mistake behind her once and for all.

"You mentioned before needing a real lawyer, a good lawyer to look over your divorce papers," Corbin began. She caught a look between him and Brax that she decided to ask him about later when the two of them were alone.

"As a matter of fact, I do," she said. She motioned toward the stack of papers on the table.

"Do you happen to have a digital file?" Corbin asked. His phone was out, and he was shooting off a text to someone. Their family lawyer?

"Yes." She grabbed her own phone, located the document, and then texted him the file. She'd printed out a copy because she was fundamentally better with paper than trying to read something so important on her phone.

Within ten minutes, she had one of the top lawyers in Texas working on her case, and Corbin had already sent the document. She couldn't help but think it must be nice to have that kind of clout and stature, but she wasn't about to look a gift horse in the mouth. She was just grateful that this whole nightmare could finally come to a close.

Before she'd finished her last cookie, the new lawyer had already reached out to her to say everything looked good, except for the section pertaining to the house. By the morning, she'd have paperwork that reflected the change. Paperwork, that she could, in good faith, sign, and he would make certain she could do it electronically so she could be done with this as quickly as possible.

"It looks like it's going to be a done deal," she said, still a little shocked at how fast Corbin could get something done. "He got them to strike the house and sign a new agreement."

"At ten o'clock at night? Makes me wonder if Uncle Keif and maybe even Kellan were making a play for this place because they're trying to buy up anything and everything they can for a bargaining chip." Brax said after a thoughtful pause.

Corbin was already nodding before Brax finished his sentence. "I just had the same thought."

Liv's cell buzzed. She picked it up off the table and

glanced at the screen. She didn't bother to hide her shock. "Wow. It's done. The paper is here for me to sign."

"With Uncle Keif under investigation and spending tonight in jail, maybe they just want to be done with this whole episode and put it behind them too," Brax said. He shot another look at his brother than Liv definitely was going to be asking his brother about later.

"Uncle Keif is in jail?" Corbin asked.

"You didn't hear?" Brax asked.

Corbin shook his head. "I haven't spoken to Lawler in a while. Guess I didn't get the latest update."

Liv stared at the screen. Excitement bubbled up as she pulled up the document, and then signed everywhere she needed to. Sending that e-mail made her fifty pounds lighter.

"I didn't realize how much this had been weighing on me until now," she said with a genuine smile and the very real feeling life might be turning in her favor.

Could she trust the feeling?

16

"Wake up, Liv. We have to go," Corbin's strong voice broke through the fog.

Liv coughed, chugging in smoke as she felt herself being shaken. She bolted upright as a wet hand towel was placed over her nose and mouth. She quickly assessed the situation and realized there was fire this time. There was smoke, heat and Corbin was coaxing her to get up and run.

He opened the second story window and shouted down to someone she believed was probably Brax. He grabbed the comforter and motioned for her to go to the window.

She climbed over as he threw the covers outside, holding tight to one end.

"Grab hold," he instructed. "I won't let you fall."

She did and climbed out as far as she could to a waiting Brax.

"You can drop. I'll catch you," Brax said.

Liv let go of the blanket and within seconds found herself landing on Brax, who shielded her from the ground. A few seconds later, Corbin joined them.

"The hoses." She jumped to her feet and then tore off around the side of the building. Corbin took the opposite side and Brax stayed back.

As she rounded the corner, she slammed into a literal wall. Before she could scream for help, another rag was being forced over her nose and mouth.

Liv blinked her eyes open as she was being dragged toward the woods. She could not afford to lose consciousness. Her eyes had not adjusted to the light. Her nose and throat still burned from the smoke.

There was something familiar about the male figure literally dragging her toward the trees. She struggled to stay conscious and managed to get out an ear-splitting scream for help.

The man turned around. His full force of attention on her. She had no idea if Corbin or Brax could hear her over the sounds of the water hose or the fire, so she couldn't count on them coming to her rescue.

While being dragged, she dug her fingernails into the man's wrists. He grunted and muttered a curse.

"Uncle Jody." She would recognize his voice anywhere.

He practically growled at her. "It'll all be over soon enough now and if I'm lucky no one will find the body."

She struggled against his grip that was like a vise.

"You're in the way. You need to go," he said. The sound of his voice was so evil and absent. Absent of any emotion. Absent of any humanity. And absent of any redeeming quality. He seemed determined to take her out and she quickly realized he was the only family she had left. With her out of the picture, the house and land would revert to him. He would inherit everything, including her small bank account. "Keif promised me he could get rid of you and I could have the house if I 'helped' you decide to go and never look back.

It wasn't supposed to come to this, stupid child. Look what you're making me do."

The fact that the place had been set on fire would cast suspicion away from him. Why would he destroy something that he wanted so badly? The place itself was worth a fair amount of money but the sentimental value far outweighed any monetary value for the property that had been in her family for generations.

The timing of her divorce, and the play Corbin's uncle had made for the property, would make them seem guilty. Keifer Firebrand seemed to want rid of her. It was awful someone hated her so badly, but he wasn't a criminal and never would have sanctioned this. Now, she suspected Jody had gotten ahold of Kellan's phone to send those threatening texts.

So, she had one choice because she knew if this man got her into those woods, she was not coming out alive.

Again, she screamed a blood-curdling scream. Uncle Jody spun around and took a swipe at her. The move caused him to release one of her arms, which was a turn of fate. It was her dominant side. She planted it on the ground and bucked as he bent toward her. She kicked her feet up and was able to connect with his chin. His head snapped back and she heard a crack, which meant she'd done some damage. *Good.*

She managed another yelp, but heard the thunder of footsteps coming their way before she had a chance to unleash. Uncle Jody must have heard it too because he bit out a string of expletives and dropped her.

He took off running toward the woods, disappearing into the tree line.

"Stay with her," Corbin's voice cut through the darkness.

The next thing she knew, Brax was kneeling by her side.

"Where are you hurt?" he asked, helping her sit up.

She assessed the damage and decided, for better or worse, it was just a couple of scrapes and bruises.

"I'm okay. What about Corbin?" she asked. Her eyes were beginning to adjust to the darkness and she saw Brax lean back to sit on his heels. He had his hands on either side of the hips and his gaze directly focused on the tree line.

"He knows what he's doing," was all Brax said. The fact he spoke with authority had her convinced he was trying to persuade himself staying back as requested had been the best move.

CORBIN COULD SEE the object of his anger less than ten feet in front of him. The man was large and Corbin immediately knew who it was...Jody. No cane this time. And the man could run. He was bolting through the trees, zigzagging, trying to put distance between them.

All Corbin had to do was turn up the gas and he would catch the man. So, that was exactly what he did.

When Corbin was within arm's reach of Jody, he launched himself at the back of the man's knees. Jody dead-legged, his knees jutted forward as his torso flew backwards. He landed on top of Corbin's back, knocking the wind out of him as the pair hit the ground. Jody's sheer size had Corbin pinned to the ground for a few seconds as he caught his breath.

Corbin rolled and scrambled up onto all fours in time to take the heel of Jody's boot in the shoulder. The kick was fired from a bad angle and came up short, so left minimal damage. Corbin hopped to his feet. Sticks and rocks jabbed into him as he pushed through the pain so he could deliver a blow that connected with Jody's nose.

Corbin withdrew his hand and tried to shake off the pain shooting through his hand from his knuckles.

Jody went on a rampage, kicking, punching, and grabbing at Corbin. The moves were desperate, but a few connected, causing more pain to shoot through Corbin in more places than he wanted to count. He threw a punch, connecting his fist with the man's jaw. He heard bone crunching. At least, that was the sound. Jody was built solid and the man could take a beating. Jody had obviously been in his fair share of fights.

By the time footsteps came, Corbin had Jody face down with his hands jerked up behind his back. Corbin's foot was jammed on the center of the guy's back. This probably wasn't the time to think about the fact Corbin was barefoot and bleeding from the bottom of both feet. All he cared about right now was whether or not Liv was okay.

"I can take over for you," Brax said. "Lawler is on the way."

"And Liv?" Corbin risked a glance back as Brax took over.

"I'm here." Those two words spoken by Liv were the sweetest sound Corbin had ever heard. It was all he could do not to drop down on one knee and ask her to marry him right then. Because he realized his life was empty without her. But she'd asked him a question and he'd never answered it. She deserved to hear it from him.

He made a beeline toward her, ignoring the pain as sticks and rocks jabbed his feet. He brought her into his arms where she fit perfectly.

"You asked me a question a while back that I never gave you an answer to," he said.

"And what was that, Corbin?" she asked, leaning into him. Her body flush with his.

"You asked me why I never married Dani." He took in a slow breath, readying himself for what would come. Rejection? Was this too soon for her to even think about giving a relationship a chance?

"And why was that?" she asked.

"She wasn't you." Corbin held his breath for a few seconds. "I think I've been in love with you my entire life. And I know the timing now is terrible. You just put a mistake behind you and you probably need time and I want you to know that you can have it. I'll give you anything you want. I'm yours. And there's no time limit on the offer. Tell me to go away and I'll respect your decision." His eyes were adjusting to the darkness and he could see those dark roast eyes of her clearly. He brought his hand up to her chin to lift her face toward his, thinking about how desperately he wanted to claim her mouth. "I'm hopelessly in love with you, Liv. I always have been and I suspect I always will be. I love you. I want to be together and it doesn't matter how or when. We can move on your terms. I'm not particular. I just need you in my life."

She studied him intensely and for the life of him, he couldn't figure out what she was thinking. His chest squeezed at the thought she didn't feel the same way and he readied himself for the crushing blow that might come.

"I love you, Corbin," she said and he finally exhaled the breath he'd been holding. "I have been in love with you for as long as I can remember. And you've been my best friend for as long as I can remember. And I can't imagine spending my life with anyone else. It's you. It's always been you."

Corbin did what he'd been needing to do for too long... claimed those gorgeous cherry lips of hers. Her mouth moved against his and he could've sworn he heard a choir singing in the background. When she parted her lips to tease his tongue inside her mouth, his chest detonated. Liv was the only person who had the power to destroy him in the best possible way.

When he finally pulled back, her expression intensified and her eyes shot a warning.

"You know this new development is likely to end our friendship," she said, her face breaking into a smile.

"I sure hope so," he said. He smiled at his future, at his life, at the woman he couldn't wait to spend forever with. He had one thought...*home.* He was finally home where he belonged.

17

EPILOGUE

Dane Firebrand stood inside the barn where he'd spent a good chunk of his childhood. The few fond memories he had of growing up on his grandfather's ranch were either in here or out on the land. News that his grandfather had passed away had come while Dane was in deep, on a mission. He'd spent the past few weeks cooling off in Virginia before finally getting the green light to go home. He came to pay his respects out of family obligation. After he ticked that box, he planned on buying a cabin on a little piece of land in Colorado, finding a horse, and staying as far away from people as he could.

A burning sensation worked through his right hand, the aftershocks of getting too close to an IED while trying to confirm it. Frustration seethed at the mistake that left him with permanent nerve damage and a military career in the rearview.

Dane issued a sharp sigh, trying to rein in his irritation. The last thing he needed was to come home to a bickering family while he was figuring out his next move. All he really wanted to do was say goodbye to the man who'd been the reason Dane had joined the military after high school in the first place. Getting away from Marshall Firebrand's manipulations and Lone Star Pass, Texas, was probably the smartest move Dane had ever made.

He looked around, thinking the only thing he'd missed was his mother, brothers, and this barn. Don't get him wrong, Texas was in his blood and he loved the land more than life itself. Being here reminded him too much of the constant feuding between his father and uncle, and the memory of an event he couldn't bring himself to dredge up. The past was the past. And that was exactly where it needed to stay as far as he was concerned.

Confronting the Marshall about his sick need to play his sons against each other hadn't gone well. Their last conversation had only driven a bigger wedge between Dane and his grandfather, last words that could never be taken back now.

Regrets were something Dane was getting a little too used to living with. There was something about bullets flying next to his head that gave him the ability to shut out the world.

How was he supposed to do that now?

To continue reading Dane's story, click here.

ALSO BY BARB HAN

Texas Firebrand

Rancher to the Rescue

Disarming the Rancher

Rancher under Fire

Rancher on the Line

Undercover with the Rancher

Rancher in Danger

Don't Mess With Texas Cowboys

Texas Cowboy's Protection (*FREE*)

Texas Cowboy Justice

Texas Cowboy's Honor

Texas Cowboy Daddy

Texas Cowboy's Baby

Texas Cowboy's Bride

Texas Cowboy's Family

Cowboys of Cattle Cove

Cowboy Reckoning (*FREE*)

Cowboy Cover-up

Cowboy Retribution

Cowboy Judgment

Cowboy Conspiracy

Cowboy Rescue

Cowboy Target

Cowboy Redemption

Cowboy Intrigue

Cowboy Ransom

Crisis: Cattle Barge

Sudden Setup

Endangered Heiress

Texas Grit

Kidnapped at Christmas

Murder and Mistletoe

Bulletproof Christmas

For more of Barb's books, visit www.BarbHan.com.

ABOUT THE AUTHOR

Barb Han is a USA TODAY and Publisher's Weekly Best-selling Author. Reviewers have called her books "heartfelt" and "exciting."

Barb lives in Texas—her true north—with her adventurous family, a poodle mix and a spunky rescue who is often referred to as a hot mess. She is the proud owner of too many books (if there is such a thing). When not writing, she can be found exploring Manhattan, on a mountain either hiking or skiing depending on the season, or swimming in her own backyard.

Sign up for Barb's newsletter at www.BarbHan.com.

Printed in Great Britain
by Amazon

69875068R00106